#minithology

THE SECRET LIVES OF CRAZY DRAGON LADIES

featuring

N.D. GRAY   ELIZABETH KNOLLSTON   TRACY EIRE

HEIDI MOONE   KARLI STITES

CONTENTS

INTRODUCTION

LAST CHRISTMAS, I WAS TEXTING with Elizabeth Knollston. I sent her a screenshot of an Anne Stokes painting of a little green dragon crawling out of a gift box with a Yuletide Blessings tag attached. I followed the picture up with, "That'd be one heck of a gift."

Elizabeth replied, "If I was going to get a dragon, I'd have to keep it. Sorry. Instead of the old cat lady, I'd be the old dragon lady."

My response? "Uhhhh.... and just like that, a story appears."

I dreamed of an intrepid older woman who cares for stray dragons regardless of what the neighbors think. I loved the possibilities that gave me. I was excited by my "original" idea.

Then, a few days later, Terry Pratchett's Lady Sybil Ramkin dropped in for a word with me and I had a "duh" moment. If you knew how often I read and re-read, listened and re-listened to the Discworld books, you'd understand why I laughed so hard at myself. Though I was not thinking of Lady Ramkin at the time, the "crazy dragon lady" idea was not exactly original.

Still, my crazy dragon lady had a story and I wanted to discover it. I could tell she was someone I'd like to be friends with.

I talked with Elizabeth about publishing together. Each of us would write a short story about the secret lives of the sort of people who would collect dragons like some people collect cats. Then, we'd put them out under one title.

While Elizabeth and I were talking, I realized I knew a couple of other storytellers who just might like this idea. They did, and they introduced me to our fifth contributor. So, we are five for this #minithology.

Each storyteller has this ground in common: We all have a love of dragons. Whether we first encountered them in dreams, or watching Dragon Tales, or reading about Hagrid's Norbert, Bilbo's Smaug, or Maleficent, they have captivated us. We are delighted by dragon stories and dragon art and dragon songs (of which there should be more).

The dragon ladies we have written are quite different from each other, sometimes surprisingly so. But they are united by the joy of dragons.

Grab a mug of coco, curl up in your favorite reading chair, and enjoy these secret lives of crazy dragon ladies.

N.D. Gray

March 2021

Camp Verde, AZ

We begin our #minithology with Elizabeth Knoll-ston who grew up buying dragons as souveniors on family vactaions. Channeling her own penchant for silver, she tells us a story about the recently incarcerated Johnny who has an unsatiable desire for metal. Unexpectedly bailed out by a neighbor, Johnny learns the hard way that one should never judge little old ladies by the face they wear.

JOHNNY'S FIRST RING

Elizabeth Knollston

WARM, STAGNATE AIR HUNG IN the jail. The single ceiling fan in the hallway was a decoration versus providing any functionality. The scent of unwashed bodies and urine permanently stained the wooden benches bolted into the wall. Johnny Boxer leaned against the rough, brick walls, his fingers absently playing with the uneven edges of the bench.

Five months and three days was Johnny's rough guess. Five months and three days of fresh air and comfort. Five months and three days since he'd turned eighteen and could be tried as an adult. Five months and three days he'd been able to resist *the urge*.

Yet, here he was, sitting in the county's jail cell. With luck, maybe he'd get off with serving just a few months, or a fine or perhaps community service. Or in reality, it'd be all three.

His finger found a splinter that refused to be ignored. Johnny jerked and raised an eyebrow in surprise at the immediacy of his blood's need to escape the barrier of his skin. He stuck the offending finger in his mouth.

"Time to go, Johnny," Sheriff Hodgins moved out of the shadows of the narrow hallway. The old-fashioned iron ring, with its three keys, lay heavy against the Sheriff's hip. Without even a glance, Johnny knew where each tiny chip, rivet, and score mark disgraced the metal. As the Sheriff slipped a key into the cell door's lock, the subtle clicks of the locking mechanisms were like thunder to Johnny's ears. Once, when he'd been younger, the urge would have driven him mad with the need to possess the metal ring and its keys.

"Looks like you might have some luck left after all," the Sheriff said as he swung the door open.

Both of Johnny's eyebrows hitched up in surprise. Bail? Who'd bail me out, Johnny wondered. He'd burnt his bridges with his mom years ago, and his dad...well, there'd never really been a bridge between them to burn. Didn't have any siblings or other relatives close by who'd be interested in him. And as for friends...anyone he might consider labeling a friend wouldn't have the money to post bail.

"Come on, I don't have all day, son," Sheriff Hodgins said, hands on hips.

Johnny sucked on his finger and grinned. And then waited for the Sheriff to frown in annoyance.

"Who posted?" Johnny asked as he stood and stretched.

"Just get a move on."

Johnny wasn't fast enough for the Sheriff's liking, as the older man went and grabbed Johnny's arm.

"Don't know why you'd waste time and money on this one, ma'am," the Sheriff said, as he marched Johnny up to the front counter. "But here he is. Not much worse for wear."

A blob of gray hair moved up and down a few times, and then its owner finally stood, revealing a wrinkled, sun-damaged face, eyes framed with thick plastic rimmed glasses. "Oh, it's no trouble at all Sheriff."

"Sam, you got the paperwork in order?" The Sherrif asked the officer moving up next to the counter.

"Right here, sir."

Thanks to the Mayor's belief in open-concept workspaces, and yearly budget cuts, the hodge podge arrangement of desks, printer stands, power cords, and free-rolling chairs created the perfect foil to any individual with a predilection to clumsiness.

The deputy, answering the call of his Sheriff, was one such

individual. The toe of his right boot got caught, and the deputy did a poor imitation of a few dance moves. The Sheriff rolled his eyes when the young deputy regained his balanced and held the thick folder aloft in triumph.

Johnny grinned at the sight of that manila folder, bursting to the seams with records of his law-breaking days. He knew he shouldn't be proud of such a thing, but having such a thick file meant at least he mattered enough to someone to keep track of him.

"Alright, it looks like everything is in order," the Sheriff said. Johnny watched as the Sheriff's eyes moved back and forth over the top leaf of paper and then glanced up at Mrs. Wormwood. Then his eyes hopped back down and re-read whatever had caught his attention.

"Mrs. Wormwood, it says here that you're the one who made the report? But now you're bailing him out? Are you trying to say you were mistaken? If so, you don't need to waste your money on him, we'll simply walk you through it again and see if something was missed."

Surprise and a twinge of suspicion worked their way through Johnny's thoughts and took a frightening leap as he watched the old woman smile, her pearly white teeth shining away. Her deep brown eyes twinkled as she pushed her glasses up with a gnarled, arthritis-wracked finger.

"Oh, no. No mistake. Johnny here was the one. Saw him plain as day."

The Sheriff sat the folder down and closed it. "Then why are you posting bail?"

Mrs. Wormwood leaned towards the counter, the unmistakable perfume of someone well past their prime moving with her. Her finger tapped the counter three times, and said, "Just doing my good deed for the week." Her smile turned to Johnny. "Come on, I've got my old gal parked out front. Thought you could drive the two of us home."

Johnny soon found himself sitting behind the wheel of the piece of junk he and some boys in his neighborhood had vandalized more than a few times. He cringed as he turned the key and the engine gasped and sputtered.

"Just crank it a few times, just needs a couple of tries to get going like this old lady does in the morning," Mrs. Wormwood chuckled as she patted Johnny's arm.

It's a miracle, Johnny thought, as the car shook, and he put it in drive.

"Oh, and let's hit the store before we get home dear, I need to pick up a few things, and I figured you'd be able to help."

Johnny threw her a look of disbelief, but simply nodded his head. He didn't understand this particular turn of events, but he wouldn't argue against it. It beat sitting and waiting in the jail cell.

Duck and Go was one of the town's oldest fixtures. The family who owned it had resisted the larger, corporate grocery stores, and despite the odds, had kept a hold on it and seen it flourish for five generations. The large duck, drawn with one wing seeming to give a thumbs up, and a permanent wink on its face, loomed larger than life on the front of the store.

The parking lot was relatively empty, being the middle of the workday, as Johnny pulled into a handicapped space and parked.

"Come on, dear," Mrs. Wormwood cooed as she struggled to get out of the car.

The normal reaction would have been to remain seated. Johnny never did as asked. He never came when called, he always waited, or hid, or simply did the opposite. Yet, his body moved of its own accord. He got out, moved to the other side, helped Mrs. Wormwood, and then escorted her into the store all before his brain could catch up with his body. Traitor, he thought.

"It won't take long, just need to stock up on a few things," Mrs. Wormwood said and pointed at the row of carts. "Grab one of those."

Again, his body reacted, his brain struggled to follow, and he threw daggers at the back of the little old lady's head as he worked to pull a cart free. What'd they do, cement these stupid things together, Johnny thought.

"No need to be so sour, dear," Mrs. Wormwood said as she turned to watch him struggle. She snapped her fingers, and Johnny about fell flat on his backside as the cart slid out from its brethren.

"Come along now," she said. Johnny glared as he swung the cart to follow her down the canned goods aisle to the back of the store.

She stopped at the meat counter and motioned for him to bring the cart closer. As she talked, he watched in growing shock and a bit of curiosity, as she stacked hamburger, steaks, roasts, and more in the cart.

"It's an easy job. I've lost something quite dear to me, and I would like it back. I've been watching you, Johnny, and I know you've got the instinct for this sort of thing. You retrieve what I've lost, and I'll make sure charges are dropped," she paused in her zealous need for red meat and looked him square in the eyes. "You do this, Johnny, and I'll make sure you're set for the rest of your life."

Now that was a deal too good to be true. And he'd heard them all. From the deals his father tried to sell at the used car lot, to his mom weaseling her way out of paying whatever debt collector called that month. And to the deals he'd attempted with the school bullies before shrugging that idea off and becoming one himself.

"Thanks for the get out of jail free card, but no thanks. I don't need any more trouble in this crap of a town," Johnny said. That was going to be it. His foot turned, his hips twisted, and he was already thinking about if he'd have enough money for a bus ticket out of the town that had never cared much for him.

Sure he'd be on the run, a warrant would be issued for his arrest. But he'd be going about on his terms.

At least he'd thought he would be. His weight had shifted forward, but his feet didn't budge. Damnation, he thought.

"It's rather simple, Johnathan Andrew Boxer. All I need is what I lost. All you need is a clean slate. And you've already agreed to help."

He soon discovered the only way he could move, was to turn back to face the wizened old woman, standing next to a shopping cart now filled to the brim with most of the meat the grocery store had stocked.

"I didn't make any such agreement."

Mrs. Wormwood smiled and pushed her glasses up. "Of course you did. You agreed to help the moment you walked out of the jail."

"Listen, lady," this time he leaned towards her, his shadow engulfing hers, "I didn't agree to anything. You're the sap who put up the money to get me out. I didn't ask you to. And I certainly haven't agreed to help you find anything."

Mrs. Wormwood's body had been a few feet away, but in a blink of an eye, she'd moved, her body now mere inches from his. Even with his failing grades in biology and physics, Johnny knew the abrupt change in her positioning wasn't natural.

"My dear boy," her fingers wrapped around his arm, "but you did. Your inconsolable cries as a baby, brought home from the hospital, soothed only with the jangle of your mother's key chain. The attempted break-ins up and down the neighborhood, never anything large or cumbersome. Only small metallic trinkets, items hardly worth a pawn shop trip. Up to the most recent, the most important one of all. Mr. Taylor's jewelry store."

Whatever bravado he'd been feeling ran down the aisles, knocked into the magazine kiosk, and fled the grocery store.

Ignoring all natural laws, and most societal ones, Mrs. Wormwood leaned even closer, her steady gaze almost level with his. Johnny didn't know if the old woman had grown, or if he'd shrunk.

"I heard you, and I've answered." Her words hit him like a ton of bricks.

"Good afternoon, Mrs. Wormwood," Brian Greening's cheerful, floor manager voice snapped the world back to its natural order. Mrs. Wormwood, now back by the cart, slight hunch to her shoulders, smiled at the balding man walking towards them.

Johnny couldn't resist the urge to shuffle next to Mrs. Wormwood, just to double-check their height ratio. He was still taller.

"Is everything all right, Mrs. Wormwood?" Brian said, not even trying to hide the fact he was eyeballing Johnny.

"Yes, of course. You're so kind to check on me." Mrs. Wormwood patted Johnny's arm. "This young man is just being a dear and helping me out today."

"Uh-huh," Brian replied. "Well, if you need help, just let me or another employee know."

"Thank you," Mrs. Wormwood smiled, "Oh, and tell your lovely wife I said hello."

Johnny watched Brian move down to the deli meats, pretending to straighten a few containers. Johnny wasn't a fool, at least not on purpose. Most of the time.

He knew Brian was just watching. Waiting, probably even hoping to catch Johnny doing something worth calling the cops. Ever since Johnny had tricked Brian's boy into letting the Humane Society dogs go for a romp around the city, Brian had had it out for Johnny.

"Don't fret, it doesn't do any good. Push the cart to the checkout." Mrs. Wormwood ordered.

Once again, Johnny's body moved while his brain, not so sluggish this time, still fumbled over the momentary loss of control.

"Oh dear! I almost forgot!" Mrs. Wormwood made an abrupt turn. Johnny just about lost his balance as his body swooped to follow the capricious old lady, but the weighed down cart did not. Mumbling a few choice words, Johnny heaved the cart around, finding Mrs. Wormwood had planted herself in front of the candy.

A finger tapped pursed lips as Johnny watched her scan row after row of brightly packed pieces of sugar. "Ah-ha! There they are!" She exclaimed and reached forward to snag a few bags of gumdrops.

Johnny raised an eyebrow as she cooed in delight and precariously balanced them on top of the meat mountain.

"Now we're ready. To the checkout," she cried as if leading a pack of starving mountain men.

"Just these today?" the clerk smiled at Mrs. Wormwood.

Johnny frowned. Just these, he thought, eyeballing the enormous mound of meat. Like a leaky faucet, Johnny's jaw dropped open bit by bit as nearly the store's entire stock of meat was scanned, bagged, and paid for in less than three minutes. And everyone around him was all smiles. No words of concern, no "I'm sorry Mrs. Wormwood but you can't buy all that meat," or, "Mrs. Wormwood, what in the world could you possibly want with all of it?"

Yet, there he was pushing a cart with countless plastic bags out to the car. And by the time he'd finished loading it all, more like cramming it wherever he could, he'd worked up a fine sheen of sweat.

"Excellent work!" Mrs. Wormwood beamed at him.

Johnny glared. He was hot, tired, and utterly confused. But ready. With each bag he'd stuffed in the trunk, back seat and in-between driver and passenger seats, he'd been preparing.

In a flash, he turned and sprinted away from the store, the car, and the crazy old lady. Three long, loping strides of freedom. That was all he got.

"Drive me home, Johnny."

It was simple. Effective. Maddening.

He fumed all the way to Mrs. Wormwood's house. Not about the bizarre way she could control him. Not about how everyone ignored her behavior at the grocery store. But how he simply couldn't disobey her. She'd stripped him of the one thing he prided himself of.

He pulled into the cracked driveway, fitting the rundown old house it belonged to. Alright, he thought. Here we go. This time, as she opened her door, he slapped his hands up against his ears and sang. If he couldn't hear her, then perhaps he wouldn't have to obey.

"Oh no dear, you're getting the words all mixed up," Johnny jumped as Mrs. Wormwood's face appeared at the driver's window. "It goes like this." And to his horror, Mrs. Wormwood sang along with him. The song, once a favorite but now on his never to listen to again list, was continued as they unloaded the car.

Johnny whistled as he entered the garage and looked around. He was sure Mrs. Wormwood had to pay a fortune to her electric company as her garage was jam-packed full of different makes and models of refrigerators and freezers.

Once finished unloading, Mrs. Wormwood pulled out two stools, and two cold water bottles that Johnny had no clue where they could have come from. Considering they'd just spent over an hour packing all the appliances with the meat she'd just bought.

He braced himself for his body's betrayal. But it never came. Instead, Mrs. Wormwood sat and tried to open the lid to her bottle. After a few minutes of watching the old woman struggle with such a simple task, Johnny huffed, snatched the bottle, and twisted the cap open.

Mrs. Wormwood beamed. "You're such a kind boy."

At this, he couldn't help but laugh as he handed the bottle back. "No one's ever accused me of that before."

"Of course they have, dear, you just don't remember. But that's alright," she took a drink. "Now, shall we get down to business?"

Johnny eyed the old woman, perched precariously on the edge of the stool. Why should he listen to what the old bat had to say? He didn't owe her anything. It'd been her choice to bail him out, and despite what she'd said earlier, he'd certainly never asked for her help.

"Thanks, but no thanks. I'm out of here," Johnny said. He half expected Mrs. Wormwood to speak, and he'd find he couldn't move and be forced to endure more of whatever she had in mind.

In a heartbeat, though, he was walking through the garage door, and out in the late afternoon sun.

Freedom.

Johnny turned left and headed down the block towards the house he'd grown up in. A house that looked like every other house in the neighborhood. A couple of decades-old paint chipping, porches sagging, and lawns giving up the fight against the invasion of the dandelion armies. The only difference was the interiors.

Most of the houses in his neighborhood had kids around his age, or at least kids he'd watched as they'd rode the bus together to school. Those kids laughed and joked, shared the story of frustration at one or both parents grounding them for some such nonsense, but Johnny knew what lay inside of them. Love. Familial love. Families that laughed, cried, and stuck together no matter the weather.

Houses full of warmth and cheer. And when the occasional rainstorm swept through, there'd always be the sun waiting to come out and brighten the next morning. Just not in Johnny's house.

There wasn't anything or anyone waiting there for him. The

cold, hard truth was that he had nowhere to go. He'd barely made it through high school, there weren't any job prospects on the horizon and he only had about thirty dollars to his name.

Whatever Mrs. Wormwood was, because Johnny was sure she was something, she at least was something that was offering him a job. And potential security. Who was he kidding, he didn't want to be on the run for the rest of his life; always looking over his shoulder. And his talents certainly didn't lay in any standard, respectable job field.

With no particular moment the decision had been made, Johnny had turned around and sat on the other stool, cracking open his bottle of water.

"I'm so glad to see you took me up on my offer," Mrs. Wormwood said.

Johnny took a long swig of that cold water. When he finished, he wiped his hand across his mouth and stared at the old woman. "How'd you make me do all that stuff?"

Her smile vanished. "That's a question for later."

Typical adult, Johnny thought. Cryptic and vague. He shrugged. "Whatever."

"A few months ago, I was playing checkers with Mrs. Olsen, the lady a few blocks down. Lives in that horrendous color of a house."

Mrs. Wormwood shuddered and her hand flew up to clutch at the collar of her blouse. "While we were playing, I lost my ring. It's quite a sentimental piece, and I'd dearly love to have it back."

Johnny frowned. "Then why don't you just go over there and ask her?"

"If only I could, dear," Mrs. Wormwood sniffed. "We had a rather... unfortunate falling out. Seems some people take checkers a little too seriously for their own good. Accused me of cheating."

He watched as Mrs. Wormwood's posture stiffened.

"Did you cheat?" he asked.

"Why, I never, that I would be asked such a question," Mrs. Wormwood huffed. And just at that moment, Johnny feared he'd seriously wounded her pride, she laughed. She more than laughed, she cackled in delight. Johnny decided he would have preferred to have insulted her rather than amused her.

"Of course I cheated. Who wouldn't against that old bag of bones?" Mrs. Wormwood said.

"Right," Johnny drawled out. He took another long drink of water and eyeballed the now crazy, old something sitting across from him. "So, the ring?"

"Yes, of course. We must get back to business, mustn't we." Mrs. Wormwood stood, "Stay here, I'll be right back."

Johnny waited until the garage door shut behind her and then he stood up, marched over to the door, opened it, and stepped out. He breathed a deep sigh of relief and stepped back in.

"Just checking are we?"

"Damnation!" Johnny yelped and whirled around to Mrs. Wormwood standing in the middle of the garage.

"No, not quite dear." Mrs. Wormwood smiled and beckoned him to come back over. As he did, she handed him a picture. It was beginning to yellow. But the subject of the photo was still discernible.

His grip tightened on the photo to the point of bending the edge. Beads of sweat broke out across his forehead and all he could hear was the steady beat of his heart.

It was a ring alright. A ring of pure gold. Johnny knew it was, down into the very marrow of his bones. The base of the band grew into an ever-increasing elaborate twist of golden strands, congregating together to create one of the most intricate knot works Johnny had ever laid eyes on.

He tore his gaze from the photo of the ring and stared hard at Mrs. Wormwood. How could she know? Did she know?

"Of course I do, Johnny. I've always known. I told you, I've heard your cry for help all these years. In the beginning, the simple sound of metal jangling, rubbing against each other was enough to soothe the urge, wasn't it? But as you grew and learned, you discovered it. Expect for what caused that itch you never seemed to be able to scratch."

The photo dropped from Johnny's hand and he took a step back. Whatever had happened earlier that day, which couldn't be explained by physics or the natural order of things, didn't scare him as her words did now.

He'd never told a soul about it. About the urge to just take anything that might be gold. One look at an object and he could tell if it was solid gold, gold plated, or simply an imitation. For years, he'd settled for the lesser objects, trying to satisfy himself with pieces with mere flakes of the precious metal. But when he'd walked by Mr. Taylor's jewelry store, a route he always worked hard to avoid, he couldn't help himself.

There'd only been one other customer in there that day. A young woman browsing a collection of drop earrings. Mr. Taylor had been busy trying to upsell her, and Johnny had slipped behind the counter and closed his hand around a gold ring before the alarm had gone off.

"There's no need to be ashamed. You find my ring. You get it back for me, and I'll help you understand what drives you. That calls to you each moment of every day."

Johnny stared at her. This was his choice. He knew it. There was no compulsion or whatever mumbo jumbo she'd used on him earlier. And he didn't want to rebel against it either. He simply needed to choose. Yes or no. No or yes.

His answer came in the form of a curt nod, and rapidly losing the emotion of surprise at Mrs. Wormwood's reactions, stood there as she beamed and had him stuff his pockets full of gumdrops.

Mrs. Olsen's house was a few blocks in the opposite direction of his own. It wasn't time though, even with the coming dusk, Johnny needed the cover of night. He also needed a few tools he would grab from his room. And while he was there, he knew he'd grab a few clothes, take one last look around and never return. No matter what happened with Mrs. Wormwood's ring, he wouldn't be going back home again.

By the time he'd gathered what he needed, dropped the bag of clothes off in Mrs. Wormwood's garage, and stood out in front of Mrs. Olsen's house, the sky was lit with stars.

Johnny found himself mildly impressed, as the only light on was one in an upstairs window. He hadn't thought a woman of Mrs. Olsen's age would still live upstairs. He shrugged, it would only make his job easier as he highly doubted they'd played checkers on the second floor of the house.

Thankfully, the widow hadn't updated her home, and there weren't any outdoor sensor lights he could trip. He slipped around back, made short work of the lock, and silently entered the house.

His first mistake was not checking for an alarm system. Any self-respecting burglar would have checked for those pesky little yard signs, proudly announcing to the world the security system installed on the house. The second mistake was flashing his light all over as he searched so that from the outside it looked like a strobe light had gone off.

There wasn't much to the search of the house's ground floor. Mrs. Olsen kept a tidy and knick-knack free home. The wood floors held no specks of dust, or hair, or forgotten morsel of food. The couch and battered recliner held no long-lost trinkets in the dark abyss of their cushions, and the walls were bare of bookcases or shelving. Johnny had no choice but to venture upstairs.

His left foot hovered just above the first step, and three things happened simultaneously. He committed his third mistake of the night and popped the last gumdrop in his mouth. Next, Johnny saw his shoe was untied and felt glad to notice it before he tripped and created a raucous. The last thing to occur was the sound of a raucous.

Johnny whipped around, flashlight held at the ready. The standing lamp which had been next to the couch was now on the ground. The broken glass slid across the polished floors, and the lampshade had been ripped to shreds.

"Please, I don't have much. You can have all my money. My purse, it's by…"

Johnny spun again and blinded poor Mrs. Olsen with his flashlight, who hadn't been upstairs, but out in the garage, sorting her recyclables. Trembling and holding a cordless phone, she let out a scream. One which undoubtedly sounded far louder and more fearful in her head, than in actuality.

"Please don't be afraid," Johnny said, "It's okay. I'm not here for your money. If you'd just go to your room and wait there, I'll be gone in a flash."

Johnny should have known better. At least after the bizarre events of the day, he should have known that just because it looked like an old woman, and moved like an old woman, it didn't mean it would act like an old woman.

Johnny stepped forward, trying to aim for some kind of reassuring, non-threatening posture. But as he got closer, Mrs. Olsen leaned sideways and pulled out a baseball bat.

Johnny froze. "Um, Mrs. Olsen?"

She swung. Not just some timid, muscle atrophied old person swing, this had some power behind it. And she connected with the side of Johnny's face.

Pain bloomed where the wooden bat smashed into his jaw, momentarily bringing the stars from the outside, in. He dropped the flashlight as he stumbled.

"The cops'll be here any minute, scumbag," Mrs. Olsen spat as she brandished the bat.

Damnation, Johnny thought. He was about to turn and make a run for it when the urge kicked in. You've got horrendous timing, he inwardly grumbled.

The ring was here. And close. He could smell it, the burning acrid smell of molten liquid. He could taste it, the sharp metallic taste of blood on the tongue. He could feel it, the quick jolts of electricity up and down his body.

The urge to possess the ring kicked out any sense of self-preservation. As Mrs. Olsen swung again, this time aiming quite a bit lower, Johnny reached out and grabbed the bat.

Mrs. Olsen looked up in surprise at being denied the pleasure of causing her would-be burglar another pain-filled whack. Johnny, too, looked surprised as he saw what he'd been searching for, encircling one of Mrs. Olsen's fingers.

"Damnation," he breathed. It was beautiful, the picture hadn't done it justice. Transfixed on the urge to possess the ring, Johnny let go of the bat, hands now stretched forward for Mrs. Olsen's. There'd been times when Johnny had felt so overwhelmed by the urge, he'd believed he could will the objects to come to him. Sometimes it had worked. He'd wake up the next morning, body drenched in sweat, sheets twisted around him, to find the object of his desire on the floor, at the foot of his bed. If there was ever a time for such a miracle, now was it.

"Get back," Mrs. Olsen shouted. Her torso twisted and her shoulders lifted, ready to strike. But the bat had other ideas.

The bat jerked in the opposite direction and took a startled Mrs. Olsen with it. Then, with abrupt movements, it pumped Mrs. Olsen's arms up and down and then twisted her from side to side.

Initial shock having worn off, Mrs. Olsen dropped the bat like a hot potato. It hovered a few feet off the floor for a split second and then clattered against the hardwood flooring. If common sense had been an initial gift of Johnny's, he would've turned tail and run.

But it'd never been his forte, and with his mind in the urge's grip to possess the ring, all Johnny could do was advance on the now trembling woman.

"Freeze, Johnny!" Sheriff Hodgins yelled as he barreled through the front door. "Come on boy, don't make this difficult."

Oh, but Johnny had to. He lunged towards Mrs. Olsen, eyes fixed on the ring. It was as if he'd tethered himself to a bungee cord. His fingers were mere inches from touching the luscious piece of metal, a crazy grin plastered on his face, and then abruptly he was jerked back. The grin melted into a frown and then a distinct expression of abject horror, as the object of his desire got further and further away.

Two of the Sheriff's men slammed him to the ground, rolled him over, and pinned him to the floor. It was over. Johnny let his body go limp. He'd failed. The ring had been within his grasp. It'd been right there. And now he'd never touch it. The urge turned sour, rivers of anxiety and despair flowing from the knot in his heart.

Words were flung at him and around him. But Johnny let them bounce off and fade into a jumbled mess of noise. Until he found himself hauled to his feet, and Sheriff Hodgins stared him in the face asking, "Why, boy?"

Johnny stared blankly at the grizzled face of the man. What was there to say? He was a whacked-out youth who craved the touch of gold and been goaded into robbing an old lady by another old lady.

The Sheriff repeated the question and Johnny shrugged and turned his head. He watched Mrs. Olsen begin to recount the evening's events to one of the Sheriff's men.

The Sheriff wasn't amused with Johnny's non-verbal answer, and all but shoved Johnny towards the front door. Just as the Sheriff's next shove was to send Johnny over the threshold, they both turned in response to a sharp cry of pain.

"Come on Evans, get it together will you," Sheriff Hodgins growled at his man who'd frozen mid-motion of wrapping a blanket around Mrs. Olsen.

"I didn't do anything," the young man protested.

"Oh, my finger," Mrs. Olsen lifted her hand.

Everyone stared at the bloody stump of a ring finger. Then everyone's eyes turned to stare at Johnny, while Johnny, jaw dropped in shock, stared at the Sheriff.

"I didn't do that," Johnny whispered.

"You've got some balls on you, to do something like that to a defenseless old woman," the Sheriff growled.

"I didn't do that!" Johnny squeaked and then yelled as the Sheriff man-handled him to the back of the squad car.

"Shut it!" The Sheriff snapped, "I don't want to hear it. Not until we're at the station and I can take your statement." As he slid into the driver's seat, he twisted around to stare at a panic-stricken Johnny. "And this time, you'd better find yourself a lawyer."

"No need to panic, Johnny," Mrs. Wormwood patted his arm.

Johnny about jumped out of his skin with a yelp and in response, Sheriff Hodgin's jerked the steering wheel back and forth before regaining control and yelling at Johnny.

Johnny pushed himself up against the door, trying to create as much space as possible between him and the something next to him. "You've got this," the something in the old woman's skin said before vanishing.

There was no resistance from Johnny as the Sheriff led him up the steps and into the jail. As the door swung shut behind them, Johnny made the mistake of glancing over to the bench where Mrs. Wormwood would have waited for him earlier that day.

On the bench sat Mrs. Wormwood, giving him a thumbs up and a big grin on her face. Johnny blanched and tripped over his own feet, falling into the Sheriff, who'd been pushing open the waist-high swinging door at the counter. Both men tumbled forward, feet and legs now tangled together, crashing down and taking not one, but two desktop computers with them.

Pain spreading in his left shoulder from the awkward landing, he opened his eyes to stare at an ancient, half-eaten donut. It wasn't the dust encrusted topping, or vomit-inducing color of what had once been a delightful, melt in your mouth cream cheese frosting, that caught his attention. Rather, it was the small object next to the donut.

The urge reared its ugly head once more. There was no mistaking the ring with its breathtaking craftsmanship, right next to the long lost celebratory, sugar coma-inducing piece of food.

Johnny couldn't believe the first thought that crossed his mind. Leave it. And then he could hardly understand the second. Roll over and crawl away.

The urge was there, the need to hold it, to have its sleek, cool metallic surface touch the scaly, rough dry skin of his fingertips. But it wasn't overpowering, or overwhelming. Not like all the other times, or what he'd felt when the ring had been on Mrs. Olsen's finger.

What sat on the grimy floor was another choice. He could reach out, take it, and wait for the crazy, messed-up thing Mrs. Wormwood had in store for him. Or he could simply get up, know it was there, and walk away.

A choice. A choice to sit and rot in that jail cell. No doubt he'd be sentenced this time, probably for at least a few years. But that would be predictable. He'd con his way into being left alone, or when that didn't work, he'd bully his way to the same goal. He'd add more paperwork to his file, heck they might even have to start a whole new manila folder just for him. There'd be someone to keep track of him for several years to come.

A choice. A choice to reach out, snatch the ring before the

Sheriff was any the wiser, and undoubtedly earn Mrs. Wormwood's praise for having found her lost ring. She'd smile, maybe push up her glasses, and she'd pat his arm. No doubt she'd break the law of physics or some such natural law in the doing, but he'd earn her praise. Praise from someone who'd been keeping track of him his whole life.

"Goddammit boy, you're one hell of a mess, aren't you," Sheriff Hodgin's complained as he grabbed a hold of Johnny, forcing him to his feet.

The cell door swung shut with a heavy thud, the Sheriff standing there and shaking his head. "You've certainly done it now."

Johnny stood in the center of the cell and watched the Sheriff disappear into the darkened hallway. When he was satisfied the man had left, Johnny moved to sit down where he'd been earlier that day.

He lifted his right hand, fingertips pressed into the skin of his palm. One by one he uncurled his fingers. With the impossibilities of the day, Johnny couldn't help but wonder what would show up in his hand. But resting against his skin, was the cool metal of the ring. The urge surged out from his belly, and out to his extremities. Tingling and burning as it seared its way through his body. Then it exploded like a runaway string of fireworks on the fourth of July. The embers burning away into a deep satisfaction.

Johnny leaned back against the brick wall and closed his eyes. Possessing the ring was everything he'd imagined it to be. With one slight exception—it was extremely slimy.

"I knew you'd be able to do it," Mrs. Wormwood's voice broke the contented silence.

Johnny didn't jump this time, just opened one eye, saw the old woman grinning, opened the other eye, and then extended his hand towards her. Mrs. Wormwood plucked up the ring, brushed it off against the sleeve of her blouse, and then deposited it in her breast pocket.

"Ready to go?" she asked.

Johnny nodded.

She leaned over, patted his arm, and when Johnny blinked, they were back in the middle of her garage.

"Rufus, no!" Mrs. Wormwood cried out.

A solid ball of mass landed squarely against Johnny's chest, and for the second time that hour, he found himself sprawled out on the ground.

"You know he's got orientation to go through first," Mrs. Wormwood scolded the heavy, invisible thing cutting off Johnny's air. "No, I didn't spend all that time learning how to use a computer, do a PowerPoint presentation all for you to–" There was a pause, and then a long sigh. "Fine, but next time you're sitting through hours of YouTube videos."

Mrs. Wormwood knelt next to Johnny and lifted his hand. She gave it a tender pat and looked at him. "Mind you, this isn't quite how it should go, but he will not wait any longer." She brought out the ring, stared at it for a moment, and then slipped it onto one of Johnny's fingers.

The heavy, invisible object cutting off his air, was suddenly visible and staring right at him. To Johnny's horror, it leaned forward. Its mouth gaped open; rows of razor-sharp teeth glinted in the fluorescent lights. Hot, putrid air clogged Johnny's nostrils. And then, it licked him.

"Rufus!" Mrs. Wormwood scolded.

"Ew," Johnny groaned and tried to wipe his face, but as soon as he did, the thing on his chest replaced it with a fresh glob of spit. "Stop it," Johnny finally shouted.

The thing froze and then whined. It whined like a love-lorn puppy. Johnny pushed himself up on his elbows and had a hard time believing his eyes.

"That's right Johnny, your very first dragon," Mrs. Wormwood said, clapping her hands together in delight. "This is Rufus, he's a golden. One of the rarest, but I can assure you, one of the most loyal you'll ever have the privilege of working with."

"Come on boy," Mrs. Wormwood reached into her pocket and threw a couple of gumdrops onto the floor. Rufus hopped off Johnny and gobbled them up.

"How?" Was all Johnny could get out.

"See, this is why we have orientations," Mrs. Wormwood said to the dragon. She sat on one of the stools she'd pulled out earlier that day.

"Genetics can be a tricky thing, which genes are dominant or not. The combinations from different lineages and so forth. But suffice it to say, you're a dragon keeper. The type of dragon you're able to work with manifests itself through the type of metal you're attracted to. That may change over time, or it may not." She wiggled her fingers, and Johnny saw they were covered in a multitude of different rings. Silver, gold, bronze, iron, and other metals he couldn't right off identify.

As he blinked, he realized not only was he seeing the rings adorning her wrinkled fingers, but that the garage didn't hold just one dragon, but several dragons. Dragons of all different shapes, sizes, and colors. Many were lounging on the tops of the freezers, a few were hanging from the rafters, and there was one curled up around Mrs. Wormwood's feet.

"How?" It was the only thing he could say yet again.

Mrs. Wormwood laughed, as Rufus threw her a look and a puff of smoke escaped from his nostrils. "No, he's not broken, it's merely the shock. Remember he's had quite a trying day."

That was an understatement, Johnny thought. But his brain was catching up. "Wait," he said and then pushed himself up into a sitting position. "Wait a minute." He stared at Rufus. "It was you, wasn't it? This whole time?"

The golden dragon preened, a row of spikes down his back snapping to attention as the dragon carried a smug look of pride.

"Yes, well. We rarely condone interference, but Rufus doesn't always like following instructions. Plus, how could anyone say no to that cute face?" Mrs. Wormwood cooed.

Johnny looked down at the ring, slowly flipping his hand back and forth. "So, the ring allows me to see him then, right?"

Mrs. Wormwood nodded, "Yes, for the most part, dear." And then she added, "See, not broken. Just takes their minds a bit to catch up."

"What, some kind of one ring to rule them all deal?" Johnny asked.

Mrs. Wormwood frowned and turned her nose up at the question. "One mistake, I make one mistake in who might be a keeper and he goes and..." She huffed, "Never mind. It doesn't matter." She rolled her shoulders back. "Yes, something like that. I know we're doing this all out of order, but come into the house and we'll go through the presentation."

Johnny watched as the dragons lifted their heads, eyes tracking Mrs. Wormwood as she stood and shuffled over to the door. "Come on then." Moving together as one, they scurried out of the garage.

"You bit Mrs. Olsen, didn't you?" Johnny asked Rufus as he stood and brushed himself off. "You snatched that ring and then must've spit it out at the station."

The dragon, his dragon, Johnny mentally corrected himself, nodded his head. "What else have you done?" Johnny asked as he shuffled through his memories.

Rufus puffed a few more balls of smoke, opened his mouth in a wicked grin, and turned to march out of the garage. Johnny watched it flip its tail back and forth, noting the barbs on the end.

Johnny twisted the ring on his finger and then laughed. Not a polite, oh that joke was funny type of laugh, but a hearty, belly-deep, Santa-certified laugh.

A dragon keeper, he thought. I'm a damned dragon keeper. He shook his head in disbelief. Beats sitting in the grungy old jail cell. With a casual shrug, he followed his dragon and headed off for orientation.

Drawing heavily on her Newfoundland roots, Heidi Moone crafts a story of small town life along the wild, wide ocean. Though she herself would prefer a horrific, Jurassic Park-style dragon adventure, with the running and screaming, she's written a retiree returned to her hometown. A stranger in a familiar land. A rescuer of dragons. And perhaps, of people, too.

WELL, WELL, WELL

Heidi Moone

THE WIND WHISTLED AROUND THE remnants of her chimney, reminding Daphne Pettifort that she was late in making tea today.

It was a more complicated process, getting from point A to point B, than most people would appreciate. Having not made the tea, she could definitely appreciate it, as she picked up her phone to yell at Dougie Milgrew.

"Dougie, my chimney's not fixed," she said.

"I'm afraid to come up there, Daphne," Dougie's voice, had he not been a grown man, might've been considered somewhat whiny. Being a grown man, of course, he couldn't whine like a five-year-old child who hadn't picked up after himself.

Daphne took the opportunity to sit back, watching the kettle start to steam and hop a little on the electric burner to which she'd been reduced. Her rocking chair—not one of the modern, artificially fancy 'rocker-gliders', no, a proper rocking chair, creaked a little, with the vigor to which she took to the back-and-forth motion.

She rocked her chair with a vengeance.

"Did you, or did you not, say you would be here at noon sharp, once you'd managed to, and I quote, 'drag me poor carcass out of bed after bein' down t'drink into the morning', Dougie?"

The groan was genuine enough. "You'us goin' to hire out to Porter Lefin for it, and he's a jackass."

That, as a statement, was absolutely the heart of truth. Not a literal jackass—that would be endlessly amusing of course, a factual jackass up on her roof—but a jackass in almost every other sense of the word, yes.

"He is a punctual jackass," she sniffed. "He is dull, but with the dullness of plodding efficiency."

"I'm your cousin," Dougie observed.

"If I peer through my vaunted lineage enough, I'm sure I could find some distant connection between me and Porter Lefin," she said. "Good-bye, Dougie."

"Wait, wait!"

She waited.

"I can be there in the hour."

"Dougie, it's closer to dark than dawn by far, and the wind just picked up, here on the hill. Is it really less scary to come up to my house in the evening than in the height of the day?"

"No." The admission came after several seconds of silence.

"Dawn. Tomorrow. Not noon." Daphne was sharp in dictating her terms. "I will be calling your competition an hour after dawn, if you're not here by then."

"S'darts t'night, Daph, you gotta have a heart," Dougie approached whine territory again.

"You have to make up your mind how much fun everyone down at the bar will have for the next, oh, few decades of your life, if Porter Lefin takes a job you'd agreed to, and for family, no less."

"I'll drink root beer," he said, sounding strained.

"There's no need to act like it's Tip's Eve," Daphne said, shocked at a sudden declaration of sobriety from a male member of her family, but the phone line was already dead. Not even the niceties observed.

She looked across the table to the captain's chair where a moss dragon sat, idly watching the one side of the exchange he was privy to.

"And what's he even got to be afraid of?" She wondered this as the kettle began to sing.

IT WAS HONESTLY TOO LATE in the day for tea, but the reason the chimney had been half-destroyed in the first place had been due to Daphne's continuing obsession with the pests of her little community, tucked away on the west coast of Newfoundland's Great Northern Peninsula.

Of course, who didn't have problems? Nova Scotia was heartily sick of piskies and spriggans, and it was said Quebec was going to reinstate the unicorn cull if the rampages didn't stop soon, protests or no protests.

In Ontario and Manitoba, up through the Northwest Territories, there was concern about whether the occasional disappearance of a hiker was due to a wendigo or a sasquatch, as the latter were a protected species. All the way out in British Columbia, you had to be mindful of walking your dogs, lest a thunderbird whisk in and make off with them.

But Newfoundland had the dragons. All manner of them.

Thankfully, none of them were as, well, enormous as the ones England had been plagued with, back in the day. Being left on an island had caused them to become all miniaturized. Daphne had heard someone speak on it a while back, but she didn't know if she believed it. Just as likely the only dragons who'd managed to escape the purge in the Old Country and make it across to Newfoundland's shores had been the tiny ones, anyway.

That didn't mean they weren't, as the locals would put it, 'a nuisance' when they were eating all the fish, digging up vegetable gardens, or setting up a nest next to your chimney.

But in all the broom swinging, yelling, and general dismay, Daphne had seen a small animal in need of, well, a little patience and under-standing. Perhaps it was because she'd gotten her degree in Exotic Biology, and had worked with Park Services for her entire career, man-aging the reserves for the magical creatures to be found in Canada.

Maybe it was because, when you got down to it, dragons were very devilish, but also quite keen, and fun to have around.

She mostly did rehabbing. If someone found an injured dragon, and if they didn't kill it outright, they might bring it to her, and she would mend their infected talons, patch up their wings, arrange for an abscessed tooth or two to get pulled (though the vet in Corner Brook who was up for such things was looking less and less pleased to see her all the time).

And, along the way, some dragons had come to her that just couldn't go back.

Marx was one of them. He was her moss dragon, and large, at three feet long from nose to tail tip, curled up on the captain's chair that guests No Longer Used For Any Reason. Probably because of the shedding of scales that took place—moss dragon scales were very pretty in her estimation, but they were quite sharp.

Marx would never fly far again. He had some flight, like a chicken, she told him some nights, which made him grumble and mutter to himself for hours. But not a lot, despite her intensive work on his wings. Releasing him out to the marshes would be a sin, nothing more.

Despite their name and nesting habits, moss dragons actually needed to be able to fly. The only dragons in Newfoundland who weren't habitual fliers were the tiny hill wyrms, as the locals called them. They had miniscule, useless wings, and chased rodents and squirrels along the ground to eat them. Hill wyrms were actually quite appreciated by the locals for their pest control capabilities.

Above her head, on a perch she'd made Dougie install a few years back, was Ghandi, her berry dragon. He was narrower than mossy old Marx, and one of the most colorful dragons in the province. Sadly, that only made them more desirable to smugglers, which was where Ghandi had been rescued from. Because of an ongoing breathing issue, she'd ended up with him, and it had finally been determined he would need to be on medication for the remainder of his life.

Ghandi didn't mind sleeping on her bed in the least, while Marx couldn't be lured with treat nor singing—all dragons, of course, could potentially be lured by singing, if you had the pipes for it. There was no worse critic than a dragon, all of whom seemed to be possessed of perfect pitch.

And lounging on the floor, over by the door, was Thatcher, chortling to herself. Her translucent wings were seashell colored, as she was a beach dragon, fond of frolicking in the foam. There were dozens of kinds of beach dragon, of course, but calling her a seashell dragon might make a person think she was fragile.

Any dragon who knew the ocean was not prone to fragility.

Just as Daphne was about to contemplate a bit of knitting before supper, Thatcher stopped chortling and started to hiss, a refrain taken up by Marx and Ghandi shortly thereafter.

"Everyone calm down," Daphne said, to little avail. She shooed off Thatcher and went to open the door, because it could only mean a visitor.

Three children of the nearby town of Hard Knock stood there. Daphne lived just on the outskirts, because of her dragon proclivities.

"Ellie, Jasper, Collin, what's on the go?"

She tried to be as friendly to the children as she could, because children were very valuable. The hate wasn't ingrained in them yet for dragons, they possessed curiosity, and for every one of them who happened to be innately cruel, another was innately kind.

Jasper, who was Penny Happensby's youngest, looked at Thatcher with wide, saucer eyes, but Ellie had been to see Miss Pettifort before, and she stepped forward.

"We found one," she said. "Out on the old bar."

Daphne was already reaching for her scarf and her coat, slinging her dragon retrieval bag over her shoulder once she was dressed for going outside. It was raining, of course, but no one paid it much heed. In Newfoundland, if you got fussed over rain, you'd never be out of doors again, most likely.

"Tell me everything, Ellie," she said, and the little girl nodded, in charge of the story, just like that. Collin looked a little sulky, but he needed to speak up if he wanted to be heard.

"We were looking for treasure," Ellie began, which was as good a reason to be romping around on the old sand bar by the headland as any. The stories of pirates burying treasure out there were older than the town of Hard Knock, for a certainty. Older than the mine in town that no longer ran.

As a child, Daphne might've spent some time looking for an errant chest or two.

"And we thought we heard something," Collin interjected, a bold ploy to take control of the narrative.

"Like a grass dragon," Jasper said, his eyes still wide.

"You didn't touch a grass dragon, did you?" Daphne stopped and grabbed all their little tender hands to check them for possible slashes.

Grass dragons, of the beach type, were actually quite dangerous. They lived amongst sea grass, which itself could cut a person like a blade, and the dragons were much the same. Problematic, considering they were also amongst the most affectionate and friendly of dragons.

"Noooo," the three children said in a ragged chorus of denial.

"It wasn't even a grass dragon," Ellie tacked onto the end, shaking her head with violent earnestness. "We went until we found Keyley's Well."

There had been a fool of a man, putting a well where he had. She nodded, and then made a quick grab for little Jasper as a good swell of wind came along. She clenched her coat more tightly.

"The dragon seems to be down in the well," Ellie had to turn her head to the side, already well-practiced in how to make her voice carry over a violent wind, and she couldn't be much more than eight.

"The well is covered," Daphne frowned. The well should be covered. A child had fallen down, cracked his skull, and never been right again, back when Daphne was about to graduate from school and go off to university. It had been a scandal.

"Got caved in," Collin ventured. And a few minutes later, struggling on the sand bar, Daphne could see for herself.

Two of the beams had rotted away, and there was, indeed, enough of a hole for a dragon to creep into.

And dragons loved to nest in caves and the like, they could fly in and out as neatly as you'd please. Unless something went wrong.

"Can you hear it?" Jasper whispered to her, and Daphne couldn't hear much over the nearby crash of waves, as well as the wind, which was still rising.

She clutched the beam that held up half the roof that still stood over the well, and she put her ear to one side, to listen.

Nothing. Then she took a deep, salty, breath of air, and started to sing.

The first note was a smidge rocky, but by the time she hit the chorus of Jingle Bells, things were going strong, and out of nowhere, there was a mournful warble.

"What kind is it?" Ellie asked.

"The in trouble kind," Daphne said, though she frowned. Usually, and this was something she rather enjoyed doing, she could tell a dragon by the sound of its call, and this one had her stumped. Of course, it was likely in some degree of pain, and probably sounded off as a result.

"Can you lure it out? You sing real good," Collin noted. "None of us can sing a hang, I guess."

"I did a minor in the Music department," Daphne almost smiled. Anyone making a career of dragon work tended to do that. "Let me think."

She didn't have good options.

She could try and pry the rest of the boards up. They were all half-rotted, and would have to be replaced anyway. But how would she ever get down a well? The gloom would be here before she could bring anyone properly, and Daphne was fit, but not, well, mountain-climbing scaling anything fit.

No one from town would sensibly try and help her, of course.

And even if they did, she couldn't send someone down after a dragon ignorantly.

"Collin," she said reluctantly. "I need you to go along and bang on Mr. Munsie's door, be a dear, and see if he can come out to consider this."

"Okay," Collin said, and took off at that dash only a small child could accomplish.

"Will Mr. Munsie be able to help?" Ellie sounded as doubtful as Daphne felt, as she began to pull off boards.

"Well, if he doesn't, I'm going to need at least one adult knowing I went down a well today," she said grimly.

HAROLD MUNSIE STALKED UP THE sand bar with his two mostly-grown sons and a frown on his face.

"Daphne, for the lovagad, tell me you aren't going down in that fool's well to try and get one of those critters," he snapped, the wind taking his words away almost before she could hear them.

Daphne, who at least did have a length of rope in her emergency rucksack, gave him the 'you are an idiot' look, at which his older son, Auggie, turned away, his face going quickly scarlet with suppressed laughter.

"Well, someone's going down this well today," she said. "I've half a mind to chuck you down there first to cushion my landing, Harry, if you're going to speak to me like I'm one of your students."

Harold Munsie was both Principal of the high school and head of the volunteer fire department. It was the latter role that Daphne was most interested in, as she held up the rope, and showed him the storm lantern tied to it.

"Ah," he said, and shook his head. "How'd you pry all them boards up so fast?"

"They're more rotted than Uncle Otto's teeth," Ellie said primly, and then she looked confused when every adult present burst into laughter.

"She's right though," Daphne said, as the dragon trapped in the well—who hadn't flown out with the removal of the boards—made another mournful sound.

"That's miserable," the younger of Harry's boys, Dickie, noted. "I'll go down, Da."

"The...no you will not," Harry said, cutting himself short with the recognition that there were children present. No one in high school had likely been spared their ears, Daphne suspected. She'd gone to school with Harry, and knew he'd been able to swear like his sailor father since he'd been Jasper's age, at least.

"No, I don't mind," Dickie said, half-bemused and half serious, from his nod to Daphne.

"We could drive the truck up and use the winch," Auggie, noted. He was going to be an engineer, or so the talk went around town. He'd had a science fair thing that had ended up at the provincial finals. The brains had flourished in Munsie's house, they said, for his oldest child, his girl Freya, was already pre-med over at Memorial.

And with her having more than half a mind to come back to Hard Knock to have a practice in the clinic, it meant they'd have a doctor for an entire generation. It was a good thing for the town, if you asked virtually anyone, especially since they were still trying to find their way after the closure of the mine.

Daphne intended to wheedle occasional emergency medical help for dragons out of Freya if she could possibly manage it.

While the men argued, she and Ellie, who'd already worked it out between them, lowered the light down in the well while Jasper and Collin held onto one another and watched. Jasper, legitimately, wasn't quite tall enough to see into the well.

After a few moments, they were joined by Dickie, who was quite able to look down the well, and then freaked his father out by leaning on one of the posts.

"You'll fall down and bash your brains out and your mother will kill me," he said at once.

But she'd found the dragon. The well wasn't too deep, thank goodness, and there was just a bit of water at the bottom. Something had caused part of the side to collapse, and she could see the dragon, pinned by its poor little wings, looking as miserable as only a desperately trapped dragon could look.

Its eyes whirled up at her, colorful like a stormy sky when the sun flashed through, and Daphne frowned, because she'd never seen anything like it before.

A rare species.

"That's no regular beach dragon," she declared. "Under the Protected Dragon Act, Harry, something has got to be done."

"I'll get the truck," Auggie nodded, and jogged off without another word. "And the ladder."

Harry came to look down, and he snorted.

"A dragon's a dragon," he said. "Why is he down there, anyway?"

"Oh, look," Ellie, who'd been twisting the lantern here and there, gasped. "Eggs!"

Daphne closed her eyes. Ah, a dragon sitting on a clutch of eggs. She instantly looked up above their heads, the thing she should've done in the first place, only humans weren't quite wired like that.

Hidden, up in the half-roof, she found the mate of the dragon trapped below, silently watching.

"Harry, take the children and step back from the well," Daphne said in the 'there's a spider on your shirt collar' voice.

Harry, to his credit, didn't argue the point for once in his life, and swept the two boys next to him away from the well properly. On the other side, she saw Dickie take the rope from Ellie and shoo her off. He was at an angle to see what she saw.

"Hello there, lovey," Daphne said in a calming voice. "We're here to get everyone out of the well, but you need to let us do that."

She held out her hand, taking off her glove, because she would inevitably smell a little of dragon, and it might be comforting.

Or, possibly, it could bite off a finger.

The dragon didn't move, but it also had the mysterious, swirling, colorful eyes. A bit like sea glass, but with more gold in them. More glitter, up this close.

"What do we do?" Dickie asked, sounding a little awestruck as he ducked in to sneak a peek.

"We either go down and hope this one doesn't get angry at us, or we leave and do nothing at all," Daphne said.

"I know what I'm in favor of," Harry grumbled, off to one side.

AN HOUR LATER, IT WAS gloomy, the wind had at least died down, and the dragon was still sitting there, unresponsive. She'd sung a few bars of Ave Maria, she'd offered some dried fish, and then some dried berries (most people didn't believe that some dragons preferred plants to meat, though technically all of them seemed to be fairly omnivorous), and finally she'd given up.

The positioning of the ladder that the fire department had brought had been a trial. Getting it down in the well so that it wouldn't smash eggs or hit the dragon they were trying to rescue, all the while not hitting the dragon who was hiding in the half a roof? Frustrating. If the entire roof had still been over the well, it couldn't have been managed at all.

A half-dozen young men were there by now. Dickie was still interested in going down in the well himself, but Daphne wasn't sure he was made for it.

Of course he was miles better than Ray Chambers, who had tried to shoo off the dragon closest to them, and still looked at it like he'd enjoy shooting at it with his hunting rifle.

Which he'd brought along. She had made him unload all the bullets, and give them to her. They rattled in Daphne's pocket in an unfriendly fashion.

"I'm literally trained to do this," she explained to the men as she strapped her miner's helmet onto her head, and turned on the lamp.

"Daphne," the one woman, Maisie, Harry's wife, shook her head. "You're almost sixty years old."

She was a sprightly and robust sixty, dammit. Fifty-nine, even. Her birthday was next month.

"I get more exercise than anyone here," she said, and with one fluid motion, she was over the side of the well and on the ladder.

There was a lot of silence as she went down. The question now became, free the dragon, or get the eggs first?

Dragons nested their eggs, but dragon eggs were particularly hardy, because dragons themselves, well, had an inner fire.

Not that they could breathe fire, like the old tropes. The bigger dragons apparently could, of course. Terrifying. But most of the little ones weren't up to it—not that you'd believe it from the quantity of 'roof fires caused by dragon' stories that circulated.

However, dragons did run rather hot, and the eggs could survive for longer than, say, bird's eggs. The dragons themselves rarely had trouble with harsh, long, Newfoundland winters.

It was still a puzzle as to why most species didn't migrate, considering a half-dozen types of ocean dragon made an annual trek from the Caribbean to Newfoundland and back again.

"Eggs in September," she muttered.

Dragons weren't stupid. They laid eggs in the spring, for the most part.

It was September. Something was definitely crazy about this entire situation.

She was down to where the eggs were. The smell of old well was quite memorable. Daphne believed she'd have nightmares about this for a while. But the question now was, take the eggs?

If she did, the dragon up top might attack her, and attack them all. But it might also make the dragon who was trapped more willing to come peacefully with her. Alternatively, if she freed the dragon down below first, it might become super-territorial about the eggs, and then its mate would likely join the fray.

"I'm taking these eggs, they will be safe in my bag. You can't keep your nest here, my ducky, it's time to go somewhere safe," she said to the dragon. And then she picked up the four eggs and put them carefully in a padded pouch of her rucksack.

She had to move nests at least a half-dozen times every year. Dragons were smart, but sometimes not quite smart enough about their choice of nesting locations. Fortunately, they didn't have the abandonment issues birds tended to have when someone messed with their nests, eggs, and hatchlings.

The dragon down below her hissed, and Daphne clucked her tongue at it sharply, then began to sing an upbeat song her dragons always liked, "Wheels on the Bus".

Five minutes later, her sturdy boots were in water and she was starting to pull at the mess that had fallen on the dragon's wings. Said dragon hissed more and more, until Daphne was ready to lose her temper.

"I'm here to help you, not eat you," she said in a firm tone. "If you take a chunk out of me, honestly, they're going to come down here and knock you out of the well without taking care of your pretty wings."

The dragon hissed again, but more quietly.

She managed to get the most offensive stone off the right wing, and lifted the dragon half out of the water before rocks thudded down again, trapping her more. Suddenly, there was a madly flapping wing in her face, and the left wing was still trapped.

"Stop it, you're going to tear that wing, hold on now!"

But the dragon was frantic, and a moment later, Daphne realized why.

She had, clutched in her talons, a fifth egg.

Daphne was quite cross with herself. How had she not recognized it? Remembering the nest, clearly there had been a missing egg. Daphne awkwardly opened her pouch back up and the dragon watched warily as the egg the creature had risked everything for was placed inside with its unborn kin. It was still warm to the touch, like a heated beach rock, despite its time spent in frigid well water.

Now, the dragon was almost docile as her second wing was freed. Then, shivering with what Daphne thought might be exhaustion, she let Daphne hold her while Daphne dried and tried to warm up her now-aching hands, before the excruciating climb up began.

"I can help," Dickie called from the top of the well.

"No, don't block the mate's view of me," Daphne advised. The mate had been hissing on and off, but was perfectly quiet now. "He might jump on your head and your father would remind me of it every time he laid eyes on me."

That was no word of a lie, either.

Finally, she did have to accept Dickie's help, however, handing him the rucksack when she was close enough, and he could climb down to meet her.

"Dickie, if anyone does anything to those eggs I will float them out to sea on an ice pan one night while they're sleeping," she said, looking right into the young man's hazel eyes.

She knew that some people liked to smash dragon's eggs when they found them. Well, Daphne wasn't having any of that disgusting behavior.

"I promise," he said, and he climbed out and vanished from her view, holding her precious rucksack.

The dragon clinging to her was very upset by this, but Daphne cooed and kept her somewhat under control—and she was confident this was the female of the pair of them. By now, the two adult dragons could see one another, and that was also helpful.

Three pairs of strong arms finally reached in and pulled her the rest of the way, all of them endeavoring not to accidentally grab the injured dragon, who hissed and even clacked her jaws at these new humans.

"She needs to see the bag with the eggs," Daphne said, gasping a little. The wind was starting to pick up again, her hands were cramping, and she had a stitch in her side that made her want to sit in the lee of the well. The men were already starting to take the ladder out, obviously eager to be done with this misery. In the distance she could see Ed Lewis' truck, and his son and daughter unloading fresh timber to close up the well again.

Here," Dickie said, appearing from the throng of boys. Instantly, the dragon's agitation vanished, and soon she was poking her nose into the padded pocket with the eggs in it. Her mate crept to join her, and Daphne nodded to Dickie.

"I can't easily carry them both," she said, "along with the eggs. The male, he's uninjured, he probably should come with me, and you might be able to carry her with you."

"Wouldn't it be easier to carry the male?" Dickie looked a little alarmed.

"She's got no fight in her, poor little thing, she's tired," Daphne said, looking at the concerned mother's head droop over her own eggs. "This fellow's liable to be feisty."

But he wasn't, with the eggs in the sack, too difficult. Her house was close enough that they could walk there, leaving a portion of the town behind to clean up the mess Daphne and her newest dragons had made.

"Where did the children go?" Daphne asked, concerned that one of them had fallen into the well somehow, even though that was impossible, since she'd been down there, and the well just wasn't that big.

"Their mothers came and collected 'em," Dickie nodded. "I daresay they'll be by tomorrow, sure enough."

"It's fine if they come. They are the heroes, after all," Daphne said, looking fondly at the male dragon she had.

"I can't believe you just climbed down there," Dickie said, and then, after a long moment, he added, "and don't tell my Dad this, but I plan to go into the Biology department, after I graduate. He'd like me to go medical, like my sister, but I'd love to do Exotics, you know?"

Her mouth twitched, imaging the moment when Harry found out his son was going to be the new dragon-fan in town.

"You could do veterinary, you know," she suggested, a little imp suddenly dancing on her shoulder. "If you did straight Exotics, you'd be working for Parks Canada, most likely. But do veterinary, with a specialization in Exotics, and you'll never be out of work one way or the other."

"Do you think?" Dickie sounded actually perked up and hopeful.

"Between the sheep and chickens and whatnot, people's pets, and consulting for Parks Canada as a vet for wildlife and Exotics like dragons, you'd be set for life if you wanted to stay in the area," Daphne was quite casual about this. She didn't want to plant the wrong seed in this young man's head. "Your father would have a doctor, an engineer, and a vet in the family. Who wouldn't love that?"

"I think you're right," Dickie nodded, and unexpectedly the dragon he was holding gave a little warble, which was answered by her mate, in Daphne's arms. Dickie looked positively charmed.

She might just have a local vet at the end of all this, and Freya could be a regular old human doctor after all. Daphne tried not to count several generations of chickens before they were hatched. There was a distance wider than the Gulf of St. Lawrence between anyone and a veterinary degree with an Exotics specialty.

Daphne herself had washed out of that program, back in the day, ending up with only the Exotics Biology degree. But things were different now, she told herself.

"It's been known to happen," she sniffed, feeling a little surly all of a sudden.

"So, where do we put them?" Dickie asked, and Daphne deflated a little further.

"I don't have a lot of spaces really suited to a nesting pair, with eggs," she said. "So I daresay I'll either have to clear out the hoard and let them have it, or I'll have to, well, sort of give up my bedroom."

Dickie looked wide-eyed at her, and they didn't have much to talk about after that.

REALISTICALLY, SHE WAS NEVER GOING to clear out the hoard.

Hoards, dragon nesting sites, were notoriously difficult to establish to begin with. Contrary to popular, and dangerous, belief, Dragons honestly didn't hoard gold and gems, precious metals, often at all. Sure, yes, in the olden days, that had been A Thing, apparently.

Just the other evening on the news she'd been watching an announcement about a new, ancient dragon hoard that had been uncovered. England, having been a traditional home for dragons even after they'd been driven out of mainland Europe, was able to enjoy such largesse, as long as they could find the hoard before illicit treasure-hunters did.

There'd be a new dragon hoard museum at the end of that dig, for a certainty. This hoard was rumored to have the missing Crown Jewels from King John's time, lost in the thirteenth century, inside. Of course, Daphne had heard that about any dragon hoard discovered in Northern England in the past, to no avail.

But in homely Newfoundland, dragons liked to hoard pretty shells or semi-precious beach rocks. They might choose old moose bones, or peat moss, or pinecones.

She had four dragons, not counting the house-dragons, in the rehab hoard currently, and they weren't liable to be budged yet. Two broken wings, one leg on the mend, and another recovering from having been trapped to be smuggled, but who had a better outcome than Ghandi, her wheezy little fellow.

Long-suffering, and knowing the dragon tantrums that were going to ensue, Daphne headed straight into her own bedroom with the mated pair, who were a little ruffled, realizing they were intruding on an informal hoard within the house, even if there were no mated pairs inside.

"Marx, Thatcher, Ghandi, I'd like you to meet the Curies," she said, formally, having decided on names on the trek back to the house. "They are having a lot of eggs and can't go outside until I've had a vet to see them."

At the least, Madame Curie needed some attention.

"Uh, what should I do?"

Clearly, she'd reached the end of young Dickie's experience level.

"Check the hall closet, Dickie, there should be a basket on the left lower side with what looks like old blankets. Those are for dragons," she said. She had already put down the waterproof covering for her bed and begun to arrange pillows into a nest-like shape. When Dickie appeared with what someone might've thought were way too many blankets, she actually grinned at him.

"Our dog had puppies two years ago and it was a huge mess," he said, and she nodded, taking blanket after blanket and arranging them into something of a nest.

The male dragon began helping her, while she clucked tenderly at Marie Curie, her injured mother.

"I am going to have to clean and bind your wing," she said. "But you won't need to go hunting, I will manage that as well."

"Do they understand English?" Dickie asked, hovering near the doorway with a couple of blankets still in his arms.

"Right now, more the tone than the substance, though you never know. Dragons can understand English well enough if they spend enough time with people," she said. "They're one of the Exotics who can learn human speech fairly well."

"Like mermaids or parrots," he said, and Daphne laughed.

"Parrots, despite their proven ability to mimic human speech, are not believed to be Exotics," she shook her head as she gingerly took the eggs out and handed them to the dragon male, rather than placing them directly in the new nest herself. He muttered and grumbled at his mate, who communicated back, with each egg that was placed, and finally he settled on them for a minute, his sinewy body curling over the clutch.

"Weren't dragons and parrots both carried around by pirates?" Dickie sounded confused.

"I've heard a couple of stories about pirates with parrots, but really now, Dickie, since dragons are known for loving treasure, doesn't it make more sense for a pirate to have a dragon?"

"I guess it does," Dickie admitted.

"Yes, that's one of the theories about how dragons made it to Newfoundland, of course, brought here by pirates."

"They only live here, now," he said. "Full-time, right?"

"Yes, we have the handful of migrating species, but they still come back here. All dragons seem to like Newfoundland, that's for sure," Daphne nodded. "And at least we don't have mermaids, after all."

"Mermaids like warm waters and tourists who swim," Dickie nodded, frowning. All children living near the sea were, of course, coached on the dangers of mermaids, though every year you'd hear about people going missing in the Caribbean, all-too often tourist children who'd been left alone in the water for 'just a minute'.

It was a good thing the waters around Newfoundland were so cold. Mermaids on top of dragons was a lot for a place to put up with.

She deftly patched up Madame Curie's wings, explaining to Dickie how she did it and why.

"Best to bind the wing down to the resting position against the body, the wing has the best chance to mend back into the proper shape," she explained. "A tight binding won't hurt them, their hides are too thick for that, really, but then you have to mind them if they take it into their heads to, you know, take the bindings off."

"Duct tape helps?" He looked confused, and she nodded.

"Indeed it does," she said, though the female dragon was distinctly unimpressed. "She could get through that, make no mistake, but it would take her more time than I'm willing to give her."

With the pair settled, Daphne went out, soothed her existing trio of stay-at-homes, and then took Dickie out to check on her invalid horde in the building adjacent to her house.

There, she changed the bandages on one of the dragons with damaged wings, fed everyone up—she had a variety of meat-eaters and plant-eaters—and then Dickie declared it was time for him to leave, in spite of the offer of a late cup of tea.

"Mum will be phoning up any minute now, I'd bet," he said. And like a sage, the phone rang.

"He's coming along now," she said, picking it up with a glance at the caller id on the screen. "Yes, the dragons are settled."

And just like that, the adventure had ended, and she had to make up the spare bed to get some sleep, after leaving a variety of food for the new dragons, to see what their preferences might be.

IN THE MORNING, HARRY STOPPED by to check on her, right around the same time that layabout Dougie showed up to start working on her chimney. Dougie didn't even accept the offer of tea, but had come with a metal cup full of coffee, which he no doubt needed.

"Did you talk to my boy about becoming a vet?" Harry asked at once, once she'd gotten him a cup of tea, at least.

His tone seemed to suggest to Dougie, who was setting a ladder to go up on the roof, that becoming a vet was akin to smuggling Exotics, from the look on his face.

"I didn't do anything of the sort, but we may have discussed veterinary practice," she said. "As you know, I did wash out of the veterinary program, back in the day."

"That's right," Harry blinked, because clearly he'd forgotten. "Can't be all that easy. You were the smartest girl in school, back in the day."

She'd been the smartest *child* in school, but Daphne had long ago let go of that. Mostly.

"If you don't think Dickie's got the chops for it, you can encourage him to go in another direction," she said mildly. "He's got a good head on his shoulders and likes animals, he told me a bit about your dog having puppies a couple of years back."

Harry looked less disgruntled now, as he nodded. "The boy was the only one home. Ungodly mess, of course, but he was quite good on the spot."

"There's money on the coast for someone who does veterinary," she said. "Dickie might decide to stay in town after the fact."

"Well, better than being a miner these days," Harry, who had been a miner in his youth before going off and getting an education, sighed and looked around. "Where are they?"

"Resting," she said. "The well's boarded up?"

"We'll do a better job of it in the spring, but it is, no child should fall down there," Harry nodded. "What kind are they? They have colors I've never seen before."

"I'll take some pictures and send them along to Memorial

University, Frank Castings or Anita Dunlap, in the Exotics department, they'll know," she said with a nod. "They are rare, I think, I believe I said as much last night."

"Yes, you did. Ah, good enough then," Harry winced a little as a clunk sounded on the roof. "What is that idiot doing?"

"A dragon I released last week, a rather large Snowy from up in the hills, decided he would perch on my poor chimney and complain about the facilities before he left," Daphne explained, as they both walked outside to look up at Dougie, who had certainly *not* almost fallen off the roof and onto the dragon hoard building.

"Chimney didn't survive it," Harry guessed, and Daphne nodded.

"Make a good job of it, now, Dougie," she called up.

"I got this!" Came the cheerful reply.

"I got, by the way, quite a tongue-lashing from the missus for letting you go down there last night," Harry continued.

"I'm an expert with dragons, and I fit best in the lower part of the well, and I certainly had no troubles getting in or out," Daphne replied. "You would've knocked the entire nest into the water, Harry, and then that's a bigger mess to clean up than we had to start with."

"And all over dragons, even if they are rare," Harry snorted. "Why do you do it?"

At that moment, Thatcher, who'd been lurking by the door, as usual, slunk up and, with a bunching flash of seashell wings, launched into the air and landed on Daphne's shoulders. Talons that could shred silver-sided caplin delicately pressed into her shoulders and arms.

In that crystalline moment, Daphne could feel like a pirate, with their treasure-loving dragon companion looking out to the horizon, toward a distant enemy boat laden with stolen gold and gems, that the pirate would steal a second time.

"Well," she said carefully, "either you love them, or you don't, Harry, but they're seldom boring."

"Can't argue that point, Harry," Dougie called down from the roof.

AROUND NOON, WITH HER NEW chimney and crown now in-place and drawing reliably, Daphne was happy, warm, and giving her two newest dragons a bath, overseen by a disgruntled Ghandi, who hadn't been willing to endure the spare bedroom in his quest for her company overnight.

"There we go," Daphne said, helping with one of the male

dragon's hind claws, which was a little questionable. Dragons would regrow any claws they lost, but that didn't make it as effortless as a cat losing a claw. "There we go, isn't that better?"

And, as she finished clearing the sand and grit out from the claw bed, a small, sparkling stone came to rest on the towel she'd been using.

Picking it up, she held it to the light, and decided it was an emerald. A cut emerald.

Monsieur Curie—she'd started to call them Pierre and Marie—warbled and clacked his teeth, clearly not pleased that she was holding, of all things, a piece of what had to be a genuine, old-fashioned dragon hoard.

"You stinker," she said, and went back to cleaning his claws. In short order, she had two more emeralds, and what she was sure was a ruby. Finally, she found a sliver of gold.

Looking at their metallic, flecked scales and glassy, gem-colored eyes, it was undeniable. This was a mated pair of dragons who probably were the first genuine treasure dragons she'd laid eyes on in her entire life.

Now, why had they been nesting at the bottom of an old well out by the seashore?

"I daresay you're going to be insufferable," she said, heading over to her dresser and taking out a box left to her by her mother.

Out came some old bracelets and pins that Daphne could suffer a little damage happening to. She then went to her kitchen, found the silverware she still polished every other month, and brought the spoons and butter knives back to her room.

Unlike her other dragons, the nesting pair took these things and arranged them as suited them. The female dragon nestled against her eggs and heaved a sigh of relief.

"And that," Daphne said as she hauled the ungrateful Ghandi out to her main living area, leaving the pair to their eggs, "is that, until it's not."

Growing up on an island in the North Atlantic, Tracy Eire was surrounded by traditional beliefs in fairies and ghosts. Ghost tours and nights in haunted hotels do not frighten her. Neither is her main character afraid of a newly purchased and apparently haunted house. Not even when one of her four cats begins to act strangely. What is it that haunts them?

THE HAUNTING OF LUNA BRYNE

Tracy Eire

THE PROBLEM STARTED WITH THE transom above the door of Half-Moon House. It was made of stained glass and wrought iron and, in the thirty-odd years that the house had stood empty, had been boarded up for safe keeping. Once the renovations had begun for the new owner, it had remained safely tucked away, surviving a thump from a massive header beam coming in the doorway, and a couple of neighbourhood kids throwing rocks in their last hurrah at the grand abandoned house. Only in the final week, and the grooming and staging of the new renovations, had the transom been opened up again.

It was red, green, and gold, with a smattering of berries against frosted glass that looked like drops of blood in snow, that glass. And along the gold, stained-glass ribbon that dominated it were written the words 'Who harbours fear, a phantom's landlord be'. Luna had only heard tell of this rumour: that thoroughly modern designers had stopped to stare, and one of the men carrying in a dry-sink had stopped on the brick walk and spat over his shoulder into the garden. After lunch, he'd never come back.

By nightfall, the words on Luna Bryne's new transom had passed from neighbour to neighbour, lip to lip, and become whispers in the college town of Newberry, Maine. They greeted her when she'd driven into town and stopped at the RiteAid to hand in her prescription, when she'd dropped her credit card to put some small supply of food in her derelict fridge, and roomy cupboards of the grand old house.

Furnished before she'd moved in as a condition of her leaving Harvey Mudd College for Bally Berry, her few racks of clothes and personal possessions had sat in the rotunda when she and her cats had arrived.

It had been dark and rainy, a weather structure that had reached its hand in from the Atlantic Ocean as if searching for a fingerhold on the East Coast of America. Luna's kitties didn't like the rain and damp. She set down the large carriers and shut the doors behind her before checking if the movers had left a litter in the foyer. It had been there, if empty, but Luna had come prepared. She let out her cats, four of them, and they immediately belly-crawled into the togetherness of a fist, like a cluster of cherries.

At the time, Luna had smiled at their milling around the foot of the sweeping staircase. And, later, they would vanish into Half-Moon house for hours on end, off on their own adventures. This was the first time she'd lived anywhere with enough *space* for them. Half-Moon, set back on a large property with its bones to a collection of rocky hills. Perfect for two adventuresome young cats, and two dignified adults.

And, yes, Luna. Their human.

She'd been ready for a change of pace.

But the goings on tonight were uncomfortably familiar. They reminded her of faculty room discussions that had demanded she keep on her toes.

She told herself so, as she sat in her writing circle, now a veteran of seven months in Newberry, and blinked across at one of her human guests.

"Listen." Johnathan Butler told her. "It's clear you have some skill, Luna, but there's a lot of detachment in your work." He tapped the paper in his lap so that it made a soft, hollow sound.

"I see." She cocked her head a little. Because she didn't see. "What do you mean?"

"It's like a travel journal." Johnathan kicked up one leg, turned it sidelong and set it on his knee, crowding the round, younger woman on his left, and causing Agustin Brown, on his right, to frown.

"Put your leg down, John." He exhaled.

Johnathan barely noticed the comment, "It's fine." He waved it away, and then nodded at Luna. "You write like you've got a check-list, just recounting everything. There's no *processing*."

"I do?" Luna blinked.

"You're being too hard on her." Said the round, young woman— young professor, in actual fact. Kathy Grindle was even younger than Luna was. She was another triumph for Bally Berry—a woman archeologist, turned teacher at twenty-eight. She looked annoyed now. "And put your leg down."

Johnathan sighed noisily.

"I'm a God damn English professor, with two Silver Hammer Awards." He held up his fingers and said, "Two. I think I'm justified if I want to give some constructive criticism."

"Of course." Luna gave an accepting nod.

"And I think you're just not emoting enough in your book. It's like reading a grocery list with an axe to grind." He threw up his hands and dropped one to smack the manuscript in his lap. "There's nothing at the core of it. This just won't do."

"It *will* do. This writing club isn't trying to win a Caldecott." Said Roberta Miller, not a professor, but a neighbour, and, notably, *not shy*.

"That's *not* an award." Johnathan scoffed.

Luna began, "The Randolph Caldecott Medal is awarded by the Library Service to Children, for the most outstanding children's–"

"For one thing," Johnathan held up a finger, "*what I said*. For another, what bearing does that have on this mess?" He tapped the manuscript in his lap a third time.

Luna blinked at the pages, blankly. She honestly felt... next to nothing about Johnathan's opinions, though some twinge within her told her that she found them unfair.

"Uh, how about the fact Roberta's an artist who makes kid's picture-books?" Agustin rubbed his face. "Caldecott ringing any bells now?"

Luna, who had seen the bright colours and black girls of Roberta's work, and felt that it was important, raised a hand and said, "It does."

"Right. Picture books." Johnathan pinched the bridge of his nose. "This is a *novel*, Agustin, and it's pretty good. She could publish it. If she could get past this block. Look, I've done my time as a Developmental Editor. Luna, this is good. There aren't a lot of mysteries solved by women statisticians floating around out there. Who was it who said 'A man who is not born with the novel-writing gift has a troublesome time of it when he tries to build a novel'? I could really help you."

Luna noted in her best, if muted, tawny **Éowyn**, "*I am no man.*"

"Me neither." Said Kathy, quite unromantically.

Roberta threw a smile at her neighbour, "I've done three more gouache paintings. You're nearly two hundred pages in, Luna. I honestly don't think you *need* help. We're both doing great –"

When the power flipped off the thin strains of Vera Lynn, that wound their way from her vintage record player, groaned out their momentum, down to a stop. For a moment, no one moved, or said a word. Each person was enmeshed in that instant where inattention flashed outward to take in the darkness that had fallen, the forgotten room around them, the sounds of the house and the coming night. Luna rose into the dissonance and made her way to her honey candle and matches on the mantle. The matchstick hissed alive as she struck it.

"Oh my God," Kathy Grindle clapped a hand over her heart and exhaled. "Luna, how the heavens did you get over there so fast?"

Agustin stuck up a hand, "I'm guessing Pilates."

It made Luna laugh as she brought the pine-cone shaped honey candle to the table around which their mismatched chairs sat, and set it on a coaster. "This is good atmosphere for your book, Agustin." She noted. "All the body-snatching and arcane rituals."

"So, it is." He smiled. "Sort of, anyway. But I know I can't read by that little candle."

"Oh, I'll get more." Luna said. Not eager, though it was surprising, for this little gathering to end. It was evidence of how much she liked this group, and the people in it. Or, maybe the excuse to be among them. She headed for the tall wood cabinet in her front room.

"Power must go here a lot." Johnathan got up and prowled the front room. He went to the great bay windows with their velvet curtains and looked outside. "Well, they have lights across the street."

"I wish the house could get up and walk over there then." Luna nodded. She set down several honey candles and a box of matches. "I'll go see if the coffee is hot enough."

"*I* can do that." Roberta got to her feet. "I know the way."

Luna lit candles and glanced up at Johnathan and Agustin prowling the room.

"You know this place is haunted right?" Agustin glanced over his shoulder to look at Luna, who straightened up and cocked her head.

"There is no such thing as... 'haunted'." She said, "The only place that notion belongs is in books and lore. In apocrypha." Surely, they understood that.

In the rising candlelight Johnathan blinked at her. "You realize... Agustin's book is *about* a haunting, right?"

"As I said." She gestured at the manuscript that Agustin had abandoned on the table, and which she was thoroughly enjoying, in fact, but had always considered a fantasy novel.

Agustin dropped a velvety purple curtain. "You know it's based on real events."

"Real events misinterpreted or misconstrued by the people who experienced them." Luna replied. Her last Harvard faculty advisor had once told her 'You must be pragmatic at all times, and never weaken.' These men, who were both quite properly taken seriously in their professions, had a luxury she hadn't dreamt of. They were allowed to believe what they liked, weaken if they wanted. And it took her off guard. She said, "There is no scientific data to support poltergeists or hauntings—the things that Agustin is writing about."

"There wasn't scientific evidence for gravity once upon a time." Agustin told her patiently.

"There was natural, observable evidence." She countered.

"The same as there is for hauntings and possessions." He squared up in the wooden room and scent of coffee to explain. "They're... not really body snatchings."

"Gravity is repeatable. It can be explained by physical laws." She told them.

"I expect that hauntings will have principles one day. Right now, we don't understand them, is all. It won't benefit the research to turn away and not look at the metaphysical world." Agustin told her, and then opened his arms happily. "Coffee."

Roberta had carried in the whole coffee pot from the kitchen. In her opposite hand she held a large metal mug of steamed milk. She stopped to fill Kathy Gridle's mug first, as she was the only Americano fan. Creamers and coffee flavouring were already on the table.

Then she stood up and dusted her hands. "Luna. I've gotta go." She sounded nervous.

"What?" Luna turned in place. "Roberta, you've only been here twenty-one minutes."

The woman chuckled, "It's like you to know the exact time. And I'll leave the photocopies of my latest book pages with you, but I can't stay here tonight. Next writing-retreat we should meet up at my place. In fact, we can go there now if you'd like." She was directly across the street where the power was still on.

"I..." Luna looked around the darkened interior of her house, embarrassed that this was all she could offer these people, kind enough to share their neophyte books with her. "Of course. I understand."

It was coming into mid-October. The cold and rain had set in with zeal along Newberry and all of Maine. Roberta caught up her coat and umbrella and listened to the conversation as she hunted among cushions and Sherpa blankets for her scarf.

"Nevertheless, I don't see why ghosts are a bridge too far for you." Kathy admitted. "I'm a healthy skeptic myself, but archeology has taught me that through most of human history, people went to great lengths to keep the dead where they put them. The more unnatural the death, the greater the extent they would go to: pinning bodies to the ground with stakes, you know about that."

Agustin pointed, "Vampires."

"That's one term." Kathy said. "But anyone who died could cause a community to fear. I spent time in Oslo and Sweden working on Norse barrows, and even a Mortuary House. To the Vikings it wasn't unusual to believe that the dead lived in those houses and had to be given offerings, spoken to and about with respect, to keep them *peaceable*. The dead could run amok otherwise, or so the Viking Sagas argued. Archeologically, the Norse would make weapons impossible to use if they were to be interred with a body. They'd place huge stones on burial mounds—even on the dead themselves—to keep them from rising again. In fact, they believed death was more a change in *life status*."

"Like Facebook status. Erik the Red is now," Agustin laughed and mimed clicking a box in air, "Erik the Dead. Status? *Ghost*."

Kathy chuckled, "Something like that. Vikings believed death *animated* people with a strange form of *life*. It didn't end them. It only changed their fundamental condition. They thought it took objects, structures, like ring-ditches, or burial boats, or these stout little mortuary houses that looked a lot like *real* Viking houses to separate the living from the dead. I mean in a *social* sense."

"You make me want to write a paper." Said Agustin. *"Viking Death and Cancel Culture."*

He and Kathy laughed in the warm circle of candlelight. It was Johnathan who said, "All of which misses the fact that you're sitting in a fiction writing circle and you don't believe in anything, Luna. Doesn't that argue there's something wrong with your outlook? That you have to change something?"

Roberta, scarf now in hand, squared up, "Johnathan, that is out of line. It is *not* your business what Luna believes."

He stuck his hands in the pockets of his slacks and looked down his nose at Roberta. "Then why is it yours?"

"She's my friend." Luna said hastily.

"That is right." Roberta turned her head to take Luna in and nod.

"Luna, *I'm* your friend." Johnathan told her. "You need to work on this, or your manuscript is going to sit in the mud spinning its wheels."

Agustin opened his arms, "If you're her pal, Roberta, what are you doing running out of here after twenty-one–"

"Twenty-four." Luna inserted.

"Uh, thanks L, twenty-four minutes?"

Roberta made an involuntary glance back toward the dark half of the house that she curbed before it could truly leave the candlelit circle. "I just need to go. It's not a reflection on our friendship."

Luna closed her hands together as Roberta crossed the creaking planks of hardwood floor. She drifted behind her friend—arguably one of her best friends since her arrival in this college town—to see her out.

In the front room, she could hear the rest of her writing circle wrapping up, and Agustin's mutter, "I told you. It's haunted."

"Roberta looked like she'd seen a ghost." Kathy confessed. "And she wouldn't explain."

Luna could hear them getting dressed to go.

On the way out, Johnathan, the last in the line to leave, paused to look around the dark and cavernous space. "Luna. You should keep a journal about this place. It might help you to land on what you believe."

"Not a bad idea." Agustin turned on the ornate wood porch, his breath puffing in air. He already hunched against rain he hadn't yet stepped out into.

Johnathan Butler paused on the shadowy deck to turn.

He popped his collar against the cold, "Consider what I said? It could help your writing grow some desperately needed personality." Johnathan hurried down the steps, leaving Luna in the doorway.

Agustin glanced from Johnathan and back to her with a sudden frown. "I'm sorry, Luna." Before he hurried down through the thickening rain to open the wrought iron gate, shut it tight, and leave Luna staring uncertainly after him.

THE POWER CAME ON AGAIN at 11:59 PM. Luna had been asleep in her room for two hours by then, but she knew it had happened overnight because the house was warm when she stirred in the sun through her windows, and the lamp by the bedroom door was on in the sun.

By ten AM she'd resolved herself to get a journal, or notebook, of some kind, and not use sticky-notes, left-over foolscap from lesson plans, or the brown paper shopping bags on which she often wrote lines and math in Sharpie before she recycled. After she'd had her abbreviated morning, she walked through the neighbourhood, a pale, straight-haired woman in a thick overcoat and clear rain poncho, the flush in her face just short of rosacea, as she headed for the nearby strip of shopping complexes.

It was cold, bright, and windy in Newberry that morning.

She bypassed the crowded bookstore, still a little put out by Johnathan Butler's certainties and opinions. Like so many times before when she'd been the target of passive aggression, she'd withstood it like the stone of a Mayan citadel, but akin to a woman in a fortress, the poison in the wells had reached the groundwater by morning. There was no way not to drink it and feel sick. She felt sick that morning, turning into the nearest office supply store—something of a massive barn full of office goods—while thinking about Johnathan's words.

Certainly, she wasn't like most people. Luna knew that as she cruised through the printer paper section in search of an acid-free notebook and a fountain pen. Getting through school had proven three things to her: Yes, she was different from normal people; No, there was nothing she could do about it; Yes, there were huge advantages to being like she was. She still awaited people with the guts to cross the floor and look out at the world from the perspective *she* had. Being neurodiverse was a convenient moniker only for people inside the tent of the bell curve, who needed explanations. For Luna, it was just being herself, and the parade of shocked faces, sudden rejections, and ruffled feathers? That was her life. It had prepared her well, for people's misunderstandings and condemnations.

But those things still felt rotten.

Being different in Harvard had been a matter of hiding in place like a fawn. She found a yellow lined pad that was acid free and lovely, and paired it with a fountain pen, hole punch, and a cottage-core, gingham-printed folder. Being different in a small town, was that an improvement? She'd come here for more freedom, and room to breathe. To stop hiding. But being different in a small town, she realized as she slowed on the crosswalk back toward her neighbourhood, that was *being* the local haunted house.

The car beside her sounded its horn and she hurried across the street, dressed for rain that had a forty-five percent chance of occurring by noon, but that hadn't come. She sat on her porch with the pad, a pot of tea, and an electric blanket to wrap up in, and wrote on the first page.

WHAT DOES LUNA BELIEVE IN?

1. *Numbers.*

2.

It stayed just like that through pondering if she should screen in the porch, what she should make for supper, imaginary numbers and their application to electrical engineering, and a podcast about Euclid.

She went inside, when she realized she honestly didn't know.

"But I don't believe this house is haunted." She said after she'd shut the door and hung up the blanket that she always used for sitting outside.

In the granite kitchen, as she waited on her boiling kettle, Luna

stood at the standing scroll desk beside the front room and jotted:
2. *I don't believe this house is haunted. After all, only those who harbour fear, a phantom's landlord be.*

Which was when she noticed Beaux.

Beaux was a Siamese she'd found poking around a leaking milk carton outside campus housing one morning. He was six years old now. Beaux was a big cat, but, probably the gentlest of her four furry buddies. He was a little strange. At night, he sometimes brought her bundled socks like he could read her mind. He had a habit of getting up and stretching before Luna's cell phone rang. Maybe that was why it struck her as odd that he was sitting on the stone tiled floor and staring at a wall. Not that he hadn't done it before in her old apartment. She looked up at it in speculation. The sun streamed in through the back window of her house as the day lengthened, a pattern of stained glass from a single circle inset in the pane painted a large golden star enclosed in a green circle on the wall. The wood there was a beautiful varnished shiplap, almost black in the sun.

Was he watching it?

Like a laser light?

He *loved* those.

The kettle whistled, and broke her reverie.

She poured her tea, picked up her cup, and sighed at her Siamese—which seemed the natural thing to do. "You've got a screw loose too, huh, *Beaux*? Not that it matters to me."

He didn't move. Didn't look at her.

Didn't look away from the wall.

Okay.

She took her tea to the front room to sit in the sun and background noise of television, and pour over Roberta's pages. The colours flowed under her hands, a vibrant, colourful harmony, as young Edmonia leapt off the pages and to life, moccasins on her feet, a basket of fish at her hip, bright eyes and a smiling face. The line at the bottom of this page said, 'but I was declared to be wild, and they could do nothing with me'. The paints were, even with Luna's limited understanding of colour theory, *perfect* for a book called 'Wildfire'. When she was finished looking at them, Luna put them all into a photo box in the tall cabinet. She'd kept every one.

Agustin's story... she would read a little later, maybe... *in the morning* on Sunday.

And Kathy's *Lara Jones, and the Doomed Temple*? That was her bedtime *go-to. Always.*

Johnathan's book about a college prof and his student? She set aside.

She sat grading papers after that.

And though she waited for Beaux to come back in and curl up on her feet, she only got the two baby-cats, Flora, who was deaf, and her guide-kitty, black-cat Hugo.

MONDAY BROUGHT CLASSES FULL OF indeterminate limits, a pop quiz, and one student with the sniffles. She steered clear of him. In the bag she tucked into her lectern, she kept the folder and acid-free paper. Its first page now read:

1. *Numbers*

2. *I don't believe this house is haunted. After all,*
   only those who harbour fear, a phantom's landlord be.

And the number three with a dot.

Of course, there were a lot of things that Luna believed in. Vaccines, for one—and her eyes followed the sniffling boy toward his desk at the back of the room. On average, adults had two to three colds annually, and it was the main reason adults missed work to the tune of twenty-two million days a year. She checked her watch. Between thirty-six and seventy-two hours to peak symptoms from the time of infection. Not that there were vaccines for the cold, but there sure were for much more dangerous Influenza.

She turned the page in the book before her and tapped the little mushroom of bell on the lectern before she set in again.

Watching the numbers and math roll out from beneath her white-board marker was peaceful. She could easily enter a flow state where the judgmental, sequential front-brain kicked back and smiled at the rest of her, executing math. If she wasn't mindful, she'd start humming. There were many tales of her doing that from Harvey Mudd.

The bell woke her.

"Da-yum." Said a girl in the nearest desk, her eyes on the whiteboard.

The first years were *never* long flying her class. Luna didn't mind. She turned and looked at the whiteboard full of Calculus and thought *I believe in investigation—I am scientific.*

In the empty room, she jotted that into her list.

When she got home, Hugo, leading Flora, was already at the door to twine around her legs. He could hear her bus, even if Flora couldn't, and they were always on time to welcome her home. She hung up her coat and walked through her house, turning on lamps and the background noise of television, and went to the kitchen to find the kitty treats.

Where she stopped in her tracks as the central heating whirred and blew to life.

Beaux. Staring at the wall.

The younger cats stirred her with their cries and she shrugged and fed them treats, but her big boy didn't budge from his place, three feet from the stained shiplap.

She didn't think much of it, with paperwork to fill out, and a pop quiz to craft from among her favourite indeterminate limits. Luna mightn't ever have thought of it again except for the fact, at three AM, when she trekked downstairs to the darkened kitchen for an Aspirin, Beaux was there when she flicked on the oven hood's light.

For a moment, Luna didn't move.

Because she couldn't.

The path fear took through a human brain short-circuited higher reasoning, and she had a sudden moment of that, during which she held very still, not quite frozen, as waiting.

Waiting to think freely again, out from under the thumb of evolution.

She breathed deeply, "Beaux? Puss? What's up?"

He didn't move when she spoke to him.

Luna only broke his fixated focus by scooping him up and carrying him into the front room with her, to sit on the couch for some late-night infomercials, and wait for her headache to ease. He mewed and rolled in her lap, and was so typically himself that it put her mind at ease. She fell asleep on the couch and very nearly overslept, because of it. She made haste out of the house with no time to ponder on why one of her steadiest cats was acting so strangely.

After that... she began to mark her Journal.

Came home Wednesday after classes. He was by the door. Fifteen mins later: In the kitchen.

Thursday morning. In the kitchen.

Thursday evening, on the stairs when I came in. Ten minutes later: In the kitchen.

Friday morning. No data.

She didn't see kitty hide, nor pretty hair of her clowder before she left. But it was sunny. She bet they were sound asleep on some sunny bed or carpet. There were four bedrooms in the upstairs, and one in the back of the ground floor. Perfect positioning for sun any day of the year, which was one of the reasons that Luna had bought the house. That... and the discount.

She was... questioning the discount a little more these days.

Because it was her short day—with only three classes in the afternoon—Luna stepped out of the heat of the bus and raced through a downpour to the local coffee shop for shelter. Rain so brisk and cold that it was breathtaking, even with her rain poncho on. The wind had blown it around her as if it were the wings of a butterfly, filling full of fluid. She was shivering when she, with close to thirty other people, it turned out, got into the shop.

Overhead, the bungle of thunder rolled toward the clap of some distant impact.

The rain redoubled its effort.

She wound up shivering on a seat beside the clear Plexiglas screen that separated her from the barista topping off the portafilter and swiping the steam wand. Steamed milk. That's all she'd asked for. Hot. Her teeth chattered as she waited.

"Hey." One of the young men behind the counter said to her. "You okay?"

"I lost my hat." She shivered.

He cupped a hand behind one dark ear, "What?"

"I lost my hat in the wind." She pointed at her soaking hair.

He took a few steps back, pulled a clean towel out of a cupboard and handed it over to her, and Luna gratefully accepted his kindness. She squeezed her hair with the microfiber cloth until much of the wet rain had transferred to the dry towel. He came back a moment later, to retrieve the cloth, which he tossed in a bin, and then hand her a steamed milk. With two complementary lemon wafers.

Then he stood and smiled at her, which was... stunning.

"You have far to go?" He asked.

"Uh. No, not really."

"Just don't want to go out into the hurricane, right?" He laughed.

"Uh... no. It's... is it a hurricane... of some kind?" She glanced out at the sheeting rain rolling down the road like fingers across piano keys.

"It's the last of a tropical storm." He said. "You don't watch the news much, do you?"

"I'm writing a book." She told him. But the truth was, No. She didn't watch the news much, outside of the Weather Channel... and she'd had a lot of power outages lately.

"Well, it's been like this on-and-off all day. Supposed to end on Saturday though." He told her. "You sit tight and we'll get you warmed up enough to go back to-"

"Half-Moon House." She filled happily, more focused, to be honest, on his big dark eyes and—he had a great smile.

"You live in Half-Moon House?" Said the older man on her right.

"Yes." She looked aside at the trim man with white starting along his temples. "Uhm.... Why do you ask?"

"I'm.... That house can't seem to hold on to an owner is why." He told her. "I've had issues with it myself."

She blinked. "You lived in Half-Moon House?"

The young man behind the counter came back with a steaming galão and handed the tinted travel mug over the barrier to the sharp-eyed older man. "This is Jimmy. He's an ex-cop."

Luna shook her hair out. "Where there any... problems with Half-Moon House?"

"Well, it's been empty for about twenty-six years." He told her. "I was twenty-two years on the force. Retired just this year." He glanced aside at her. "Police work is hard on the body."

"I can only imagine." She told him and sipped the steamed milk.

He chuckled. "Yeah. To answer your questions. There were calls about your house. That house is... it's older than most of Newberry. It used to be in the country, you know? Before Newberry expanded up here. They squeezed in on around it using some Easement law or other, but you'll notice you have twice the land to either side of Half-Moon as anyone else, and the big cliff face and foothill out back? Technically yours."

"No," she shook her head. "That can't be." It was impossible for the price she'd paid to have such a large package of land.

"Yep." Jimmy nodded at her. "Maybe the city isn't one hundred percent clear on it, but I've seen the zoning for that property, I saw it when I was new to the force and we were looking into noise complaints from the neighbours."

"Noise?" She shook her head. "But it would have been empty by the time you joined the force, how could there be... noise?"

"Yeah." He nodded in her direction. "See, that's the thing. That's why we looked at the map. We had to get our heads around how much space we were dealing with when we went in on calls. You wouldn't have believed the rumours. That a mutant lived in the attic. That there were devil worshipers in the yard. That there was a subterranean cave system. Just... it was a four-person job to check on a complaint, the property was that big and overgrown. Easily. But we'd get up there with six of us, sometimes. Or more. There were rumours of parties up on the foothills, and lights going through the abandoned house. I swear, sometimes I could just about hear people chatting, or even calling out to each other. Everything. Even babies crying. But the house? There was never anyone *in* it, and there hadn't been anyone in it for a couple of years. The owners both passed away inside, *hours* apart. No family we knew of. This went on for... *years. Years and years.* Got to the point where, at night, when the complaints came, a few of us would bring our rookies up to check it out, and just watch which of 'em would ring out in the next few days. But we'd never go on the property. I wouldn't go now, either. Not if I had two full S.W.A.T. teams and the Popemobile."

She swallowed hard. *"Babies... crying?"*

Jimmy nodded at her. "Yeah. But, *hey,* I can't believe I'm getting to meet the new owner! Lady, if anyone *ever* said you weren't brave? Well, up theirs." He held up his travel mug in salute. Then the ex-cop drifted into the coffee shop crowd to check the number of the bus arriving through jets of water.

Luna spun back around, wide-eyed. Behind the counter, the smiling young man's brows went up on his forehead, and he nodded. "Yeah. Jimmy. Great stories, right?"

She felt numb with surprise. That had been a police officer. That story had spanned much of his career. "Yeah.... Jimmy.... I've got to go."

"Come again soon." He called after her.

The rain had slackened when she went outside. Distant thunder still cracked and churned somewhere in the foreboding clouds off to her left and above.

The storm ushered in an early darkness with it, and the wind batted her like the paw of some huge beast, into the rhododendrons outside of Margo Carpenter's.

And nearly into the fence across the street from Roberta's— whose Tudor looked distant through the silvery rain that had begun sheeting as she arrived back home.

Slowly, Luna turned in the rain to look up and up the lot... at the great Folk Victorian edifice that was Half-Moon House.

Oh-boy.

"Don't be foolish now, Luna." She told herself as she unlatched the gate. "You've been living in it for months and there's been noth-ing— almost nothing—at all to report."

She came through the door to find Flora alone, her big blue eyes beseeching for treats, which she was perfectly willing to throw her sinuous body around on the rug to get. Almost immediately Luna felt silly. She smiled, knelt down, reached for her cat, and the lights went with an audible click.

Flora, purring loudly as a consequence of once having had *a little* hearing, and being determined to be heard, didn't stop for a moment. She rolled her tiny feline body around, happily on the mat that Luna had vacuumed just that Sunday.

When things had still been normal.

"Nothing isn't normal. That must have been a breaker." Luna exhaled the sudden tension. She rose and nodded.

It had been a bit strained around here with Roberta running out and Beaux acting so... strangely, but nothing that deserved this kind of anxiety. She shoved past her misgivings and went down the long hall toward the garage in the gloom. To do so, she passed the open pocket doors to the parlour on her left, a closet on her right, an empty piano room to the left, and a deserted smoking room on the right. The door to the garage add-on, all in white brick, was sticky. She wrapped her hand around the handle and had to jog it a few times before she could get it to come loose, and the door to admit her. The large garage was empty, swept, and dark. Luna had to feel her way along the enclosure's sideboard to find the flashlight she always left there. She'd done this very thing dozens of times before, but really didn't want to do it today.

Thanks so very much, Jimmy.

Click and clack at the breakers, as she did, when she looked down the hall from the doorway that had once been a servant's entrance, there was never any light. She gave up after a few minutes of wrenching and trotted out of the cold, back into the house, backtracking to shut the door. She lit the oversized fireplace in the front room and glanced at the television enviously. She could really have used a little company.

Luna glanced at the door. Roberta.

She could go visit Roberta!

And... and what? Come back to this darkened house deeper in the night?

She texted her friend: *Breakers blown. Trying to fix. Don't suppose you could come help*? She almost added 'ha-ha'. What person in their right mind would hear a story like Jimmy's, no doubt stored away in some recess of collective consciousness in the neighbourhood, and then decide to pop over when things were getting weird.

Luna put the phone in her pocket, and sighed.

She knew she was being silly.

A walk would clear her head.

She picked up her rain poncho and purse and made for the door.

Her hand was on the knob when Beaux yowled from the kitchen.

At first, her brain couldn't place the sound, because he cater-wauled so seldomly, but then, heart hammering, she knew it for what it was.

He was calling out to her.

Beaux only did that... when he needed her.

But she was sure he was fine. He'd be fine.

For a half an hour's walk.

Her hand tensed to turn the brass knob.

Beaux yowled again.

Luna stood at the door—she swore in recollection—for whole minutes.

When he yowled again, her hand fell away and she turned.

When Beaux had been little enough to fit in her hand, and she'd found him, he'd been so afraid, he'd tried to run, not around the brick Residence in whose yews he'd been lurking, but straight through the wall. He'd just huddled there in plain sight, frozen, with his face turned away. She set down her purse. She was going into the kitchen.

That would be where he'd be.

Her legs felt heavy as she moved them, but they obeyed anyway. She passed through the living room, with its dead power, cracking fire, and deep shadows. And came to the arch to the kitchen. Luna braced herself and stepped inside.

Beaux sat staring at the wall.

But then, they all did.

Beaux and Hugo, side by side. Flora, who couldn't hear. And the wildest of all her feline housemates, Beauty, the slinky Russian Blue. In fact, it was only Beauty who turned her head to look in Luna's direction. They all sat staring at the wall.

Minutes passed.

Beaux made a plaintive yowl, but didn't move or look away.

Luna, arms tight around her sweater vest, felt her hair prickle.

And then... twigged.

Flora.

Only Flora had been there to meet her.

She ran to the garage.

Inside, there leaned a few tools that had been left behind by whomever had kept the grounds before she'd moved in. Among them was a spade headed shovel. Relatively clean, the business end terminated in what was nearly a point. It was something of a chevron on a steel handle. She caught it up now and ran back the way she'd come.

Lightning peeled overhead as she ran by the parlour, and she rounded the corner to a nearly serpentine hiss of rain.

As she made the kitchen, she didn't slow, but she raised the spade head up in a big arc above her head.

Beaux yowled and the shovel came down.

It lodged in the wall between one shiplap board, and another.

Cats scattered as she wrestled with getting the wood down. It wasn't a matter of a few minutes either. Beaux and the clowder loafed, chewing a third round of treats, in the sound of heavy weather, as she sweated, red in the face, and wrenched the last of the shiplap off. It was fully dark by then, and a flash of lighting threw light through the kitchen window, and lit up what had been a wall, with a green circle, inlaid with a gold star.

But was now... a door.

She took her flashlight in her pocket, and gripped it in her teeth, raised the spade-head shovel, and walked into the cold darkness of... a downstairs she hadn't realized she had. The old, stoned-in footprint of her house was windowless, with only a few grilled air-holes, no bigger than a coffee cup. In the corner, though, there was a small, glowing object.

Luna edged toward it only to find... the corner, though shored up on mortared rock, was no longer perfect. There was a little gap, just large enough that a person might squeeze through, if they were... crazy. Which she, apparently, was.

The light came from there.

And she just *had to know.*

Beyond... was a dark hollow into which she didn't dare venture. It was quiet and occasionally traced with motes of light she wasn't sure... weren't happening inside her brain rather than in the air. When she backed out, she kicked something free in the little passageway, and winced, afraid the corner of the house would come down around her ears.

But it didn't.

Something did make a... pathetic little bawling.

It was only then she realized all her cats could be down here in this soil-floored foundation. She shone her light around the floor in the darkness and the light glinted. She found... what looked like an egg made of crystal. It was larger than turkey eggs she'd cooked. She pulled in a gasp and shone her light not into the cavern, but along the walls of the basement. They glinted and glowed with what had to be the most remarkable collection of natural crystals she'd ever seen. It was like a New Age shop along the side wall, where someone had put up simple wire shelves and set wood bowls that were filled with crystal.

She muttered, "What's the purple one? Amethyst or tourmaline?"

She brought the thing back upstairs through the... the new door into her kitchen. She shut and leaned on that door and considered the large egg of crystal in the lightning beyond her window. Luna looked at the planks she'd pulled off, neatly leaned against the wall, and realized they'd never been fastened all that tightly.

"I bet people have been in and out of that treasure trove before." She sighed. "The owners had a fortune in natural crystal hidden away down there. Who knows how much was there before I guess... people got in and started taking it?"

She set the stone on the table and went to the study to bring out some books she had on gemology and geology.

Half an hour later, she sat amid candles, blanket around her, and hammer in hand.

Gravely, the cats sat staring at her, Beaux from the chair across the table.

"Bear with me." She waggled the little cross-peen hammer, which had been the only hammer in the garage. "I think... it's a geode. They come in pinkish and purple. I checked, you guys. I'm just going to give it a tap."

There was a little seam along the top already and, setting the base on the table, she gave that narrower top a little... smack.

The geode fell in two, her hand holding the side she could see, the rest rolling open and falling to the floor.

Where it gave a soft cry.

She counted whiskers.

No.... Her clowder was accounted for, if *curious*.

Beaux skulked over closer, with Beauty behind him.

The next cry was softer, like the gurgle of a baby.

Luna gripped the hammer, released the geode, and leapt to her feet in her candlelit kitchen. *What in the hell was that?*

With a great groan under the lightning and weather, the heat kicked in and Luna scrambled to turn on the kitchen light.

There... on the floor, curled and shivering, all its feathers wonky and misshapen, its little bird-like neck pulled tight to it and its eyes squeezed shut against the light, was... something she'd never seen before.

Something with long plumed wings.

And four little bird's feet.

And large, translucent butterfly wing ears that flittered a few times, and then laid back flat and just a little... out to the sides. This new thing was brilliantly violet, gold, and fuchsia, and cracked opened a large almond-angled eye to Look At Her. She saw only a flash of bright green, with a golden star-shaped pupil, before it pulled into the tightest ball it could possibly *muster*, and made a whimpering cry that was not unlike an infant's.

Luna's fear evaporated.

Poor little thing.

It was pretty. Even... beautiful with its big eyes and long, little face.

"Beaux, this is what you wanted me to see." She said with certainty. She didn't even know what it was, curled up in the most glorious blanketing of colours and bandings and spots. It was too batlike to be a bird. To birdlike to be a bat. With four legs like a cat. And a fox-face.

There's got to be a name for something like this.

"Hey there." Luna said and crouched down to extend a hand to it.

It bunched up tighter and shivered.

She shook her head, "Ohp! Relax. I'm... I'm different too. You're safe with me."

But when she spoke, it made a pitiful little wail.

What should she do with it? It didn't belong with people, for sure.

Call the pound? Call the... zoo?

It had come out of a... geode?

What was it, and where did it belong?

When she reached for it again, it didn't cry out, or resist. It turned its head away toward the stone-flagged floor, and Luna felt a familiar pity that was like steel rising up inside. No one. That's who she'd call. No one would take this... thing from its home. He was safe. Safe and sound in this haunted house of hers.

That he was haunting.

"I knew I wasn't going crazy." She told it as soothingly as she could. "I knew it was real because Flora couldn't hear you. She's deaf."

Beauty crept in to snuffle the top of the thing's feathery head.

It reached up a tenuous little hand from under its curled wing... and pushed her nose away. But it didn't do any harm to the cat.

That made Luna smile.

She was careful when she picked it up and set it on the table. It bundled there, only relaxing when she put a kitchen hand-towel over it. Then its big green, gold starred eyes stared out at her curiously, little different than how Hugo or Flora looked at her. It watched Beaux and Beauty coil around her feet and legs, and seemed to relax a little.

She made it tea.

She made it bacon.

"Come on. *Everything* likes bacon. Or... so I hear."

Nope.

It ate a head of leftover grilled cauliflower and two cuties, before it curled up and went to sleep in her blown glass kitchen centerpiece.

Luna sat writing in her journal, where she named him... her... *it* 'Petrichor' after the soft waft of rainy garden scent through the window as the little thing slept.

The list was growing longer, the more she and the cats

stared at the little... dragon... thing. The more the cats snuffled it, Luna heated towels in the drier for it, and it slowly expanded its territory from kitchen centerpiece to kitchen... table.

WHAT DOES LUNA BELIEVE IN?

She was on bullet eighty-seven, at the moment.

Bullet eighty-six had been: *Surprises.*

Bullet eighty-five? *Cryptids.*

And eighty-four? *Dragons.*

She stuck her head on her chin to watch Petrichor snore. Safe. Safe enough to *sleep.* It made a little purring sound that lulled even Beauty, but *still* with elements like a child's voice, as though it was *designed* in a way that would protect it from human beings like her. The little creature was *fantastic. Fascinating.* Also? Well... adorable. And.... And at her current rate, she didn't think she'd be finished her list tonight.

She was a *little* uncertain her *pop quizzes* would get graded.

Maybe by Monday?

The little dragon-thing hiccupped a tiny... *spark.*

Luna's jaw dropped and she smothered a laugh.

She looked at the happy face she'd drawn beside eighty-seven.

Yeah. Maybe not for a while.

A little after dawn, Roberta texted: *OMGosh! I'm sorry! Just seeing this + OTW!* The little buzz had woken her up in the kitchen.

Petrichor was, by now, on her nice, warm lap, one little bird-fist bundled in a towel.

Beaux woke up from the bundled cats and stretched a little too late for the phone this time, but heading for the front door.

Luna thought of the brightly coloured art. "Roberta's gonna love you."

Karli Stites loves the endless possibilities inherent in dragon stories. Twisting the theme of the #minithology in an unexpected direction, she gives us Esme, a dragon lady who is a bit crazy, a bit insecure. An outsider even among her family and friends. But uniqueness is strength, and on a chance adventure, Esme discovers she might be very strong indeed.

THE EVOLUTION OF ESME

A PRELUDE TO OBSIDIANFIRE

Karli Stites

"Hi, I'm Esme."

No, you're not. I smiled, deliberately ignoring the voice in my head.

Elias looked confused. "I thought your name was Esmerelda?"

The voice inside my head snorted. ***I told you so***, it taunted.

I gritted my teeth in annoyance. *I thought you were supposed to be supportive*, I shot back. *Protect me and stuff.*

Not when you're being stupid, it answered. ***And incorrect***.

I refocused on Elias and his adorably puzzled face. Maybe adorable wasn't the right word though... Especially not when he was questioning my name.

"No, my name is Esme," I corrected.

"Okay…" He still seemed unconvinced. I resisted the urge to sigh in frustration. I tried to cut him some slack. I really did. After all, my mother invited him over to meet Esmerelda Obsidianfire, a high-ranking Drakonae female born into the Warrior class. Instead, he met Esme.

I smiled more genuinely. "It's a nickname," I explained. "I gave it to myself. Esmerelda is such a long name. Very stuffy."

"Oh." He paused. "Can you really give yourself a nickname?"

The voice snorted again. *No*.

"Yes," I insisted. "Since I did. Everyone calls me Esme."

No one calls you Esme.

"Interesting," He commented.

"Yes, it is quite interesting." I smiled. This time it wasn't genuine. "But do you know what's not interesting? This conversation."

Elias looked stunned. He sputtered a few times.

"Sorry, but I have somewhere I need to be. Like, anywhere but here actually. It was nice to meet you." I curtsied, as was appropriate when meeting a royal of his rank. "Please feel free to see yourself out. Have a great day!"

I sprinted out of the gardens before Elias could gather his wits and call me back. Technically, I didn't have the authority to dismiss him from my company. Since he was a potential suitor, he had the right to court me. I was required to attend at least one outing with him. Escorted, of course, as was proper. I peeked at my chosen escort as he chased me out of the main gardens and into the hedge maze. I smiled and picked up the pace.

He caught me in less than a minute.

I laughed wildly. "Shit!"

"You're getting faster, Esme."

I told you everyone calls me Esme, I taunted. I telepathically stuck out my tongue. Is that possible? Pretty sure it was.

He's literally the only person in all of Drakon that calls you Esme.

Did you just roll your eyes at me? I asked suspiciously.

Yes.

"Still not fast enough to beat you, Leo," I panted.

"True," He admitted. "But I've been training my whole life. You only started a couple years ago. You've come a long way. I'm proud of you."

I smiled and fluffed my hair. I might have even flipped it a little bit. Leo chuckled. *Shit. He totally noticed.*

You weren't exactly discreet, Esmerelda.

Don't call me that, I pouted.

It's your name.

Is not, I retorted.

"Thank you so much, Leo. You don't know how much this means to me."

"Of course, Esme. I want you to feel safe," he smiled.

"I wish Lochlan felt the same way. I wish I could show him what I could do! He was so angry when I asked him to train me though."

"He's just scared for you. He's your big brother and he wants to protect you himself."

I rolled my eyes. "Lochlan isn't scared of anything. And you always defend him, Leo. Just because he's your best friend doesn't mean he's always right."

He sighed. "He's not. That's why I decided to train you. I don't entirely agree with the way females are treated in Drakonae culture. Sure, some of them love being put on a pedestal and married off to royalty. Maintaining peaceful relationships between different Drakonae bloodlines is crucial to the continued existence of our society. We don't want to spiral into an all-out war between kingdoms again. But I know there are probably other females like you who don't want that lifestyle. And I want you to have everything you want in life, not be stuck married to some idiot like Elias." Leo looked particularly put out by the last bit.

Oh, my Drakoni gods, is Leo jealous? Why does that please me so much?

I could practically feel the eyes rolling in the back of my head.

Because you're a psycho. And totally in love with Leo. Obviously.

What! Am not! My protests were almost screeches.

"Thank you for believing in me, Leo," I smiled at him. Angelically.

Snort. **You're no angel, Esmerelda.**

My name is Esme!

"Of course, Esme. I'll always believe in you."

We stared at each other for a couple minutes without speaking. Just smiling. I examined him. His eyes were a gorgeous violet, perfectly matching the pretty jewel in the center of his forehead. Although, I doubted he would appreciate me calling it pretty. Those features were similar to mine, but my eyes and jewel were turquoise. I was comfortable calling mine pretty. Leo was also of clan Obsidianfire, so he had the same pitch-black hair as me. Technically, it was *obsidian*. And like every other Drakonae in my clan, he was a fire dragon. Hence, the name *Obsidianfire*. Well, except for me. I was an *ice dragon*. Because of course I was—a bonafide freak to be honest.

Leo cleared his throat when he noticed how close we were.

"So, do you think Elias will call?"

I snorted and then we both busted into laughter.

"Esmerelda."

Oh no. Shit shit shit shit shit.

"I just spoke with Elias. He was very disturbed by your behavior earlier today. I cannot believe that you would be so crude and inappropriate." She sighed. "Honestly, I should have expected this. You've always been quite rebellious. But I thought you would take this process a bit more seriously, though. It's your future, after all."

"Mother, I'm sorry. However, in my defense, he was quite awful."

Lady Cassandra Obsidianfire gasped. Quite dramatically, I might add.

"Esmerelda!"

I sighed. "I'm sorry, mother. He wasn't very nice, though."

She pursed her lips. "Well, that's too bad. Hopefully he improves his behavior for next time."

My mouth dropped open in horror. "Next... time?"

My mother at least had the decency to look contrite. "Yes, Elias would like another chance. You didn't even allow him five minutes, Esmerelda. I'm sure he's a perfectly respectable Drakonae male."

I gritted my teeth. "Mother, please."

She narrowed her eyes. "You won't be getting out of this, Esmerelda. And you'll spend at least three hours with Elias. This time you'll be going to his estate, so you won't be able to escape so easily. I'll make sure that Leo knows he'll have to keep an eye on you. He's doing you a favor by being your escort on his time off. Don't embarrass him by cutting out early again. And please do *not* embarrass this family again. Elias comes from a well-respected family and you're *very* lucky he's giving you a second chance."

My mother didn't look like she was messing around, so I held back the words I wanted to say. And what I wanted to do. Which was kick and scream and rage. Stomp around. Maybe cry a little. Definitely burst into dragon form and fly around for hours. Then, I would return and have a reasonable conversation as to why I should never have to spend another minute in the presence of Elias Emeraldice. *The perfect plan.*

That's a terrible plan.

Oh, you're back, I stated dryly. *Although, I don't remember asking for your commentary.*

Doesn't mean I shouldn't offer it when you have a crazy ass plan. Like this one. This is exactly why you have no friends.

What! I have friends! I cried in outrage.

Not really...

"Esmerelda." My mother sounded exasperated like usual. "Are you even listening to me?"

"Oh, yes. I apologize, mother. I was just thinking of how sorry I was for my behavior earlier with Elias. Determining the best way to make it up to him as a matter of fact."

She looked suspicious. As she should be. "Okay, then. Please do make sure to be on your best behavior. You'll be meeting with him tomorrow. Leo will escort you to his estate for lunch. Be ready on time. And don't forget—three hours *minimum*."

"Yes, mother." *Hmm, how can I get out of this?*

You can't.

I'm sure I can think of something, I insisted.

She smiled. "Now off with you. Go fly around and let off some energy. You're practically bouncing on your toes and it's making me anxious."

I curtsied and hurried off at once, happy to do her bidding. "Bye! See you at supper!"

It only took me five minutes to reach the clearing where I always changed forms. My four bonded Drakoni touched down and joined me at last. My lips twitched, but I put my hands on my hips and narrowed my eyes in annoyance.

Like myself in dragon form, my Drakoni were a gorgeous pure black with bright turquoise eyes. Unlike me, they were missing the jewel in the center of their foreheads. It was the only thing that made our faces truly distinguishable in dragon form. Our bodies were of similar shape and size. We looked practically identical when we laid our wings against our backs. When we flew, though, it was a different story. Wings were as unique as a fingerprint. Each of my Drakoni had beautiful wings.

There was Star, who had sparkly wings that twinkled like the brightest star. Sky, who had pretty light blue wings that resembled a clear summer day. Sun, who had golden wings that shined with an inner light and actually made me feel warmth on my skin. And finally, there was Spirit. She was... *spirited.* Quite the spitfire. *Really annoying.*

You're calling me annoying? Please.

"Someone's extra chatty today," I observed.

Spirit rolled her eyes. *Your thoughts have been clogging up the bond.*

"You comment on literally everything I do."

Because everything you do is ridiculous.

"Is not."

Is too.

"Is not."

Is too.

"Whatever, Spirit. I'm not arguing with you right now. I want to fly."

Good idea. I could stretch my wings.

"You've been *stretching* your wings all day," I pointed out.

She shrugged. I shook my head. Spirit was entirely too human for a Drakoni.

I'm a dragon. I'm meant to fly.

"Okay, well, let's go then."

Let's.

"Time to get naked!"

You're crazy. Just shift.

"I'm not crazy. Getting naked is essential. This is a new dress. I don't want to ruin it by doing a premature shift for no reason. You vetoed my earlier plan anyway so no emergency shifts are necessary. I'm doing this the old-fashioned way." I undressed as I spoke. It was difficult to undo the laces on my dress, but I managed it in a graceful—*almost*—maneuver.

That wasn't anywhere close to graceful.

"Okay, Spirit, once again, you've been very *un*helpful."

I shot her a scathing look when I was done and seconds later, I shifted. *Damn I am one cool ass dragon.*

If you're done admiring yourself, can we fly now?

Yeah, yeah, let's go. I looked to my other Drakoni who remained silent as usual. They were never really much for conversation. In fact, most Drakoni weren't. Spirit was unique that way. Like me. It's why we made just a great pair. *Are you three ready?*

They simply nodded. I sighed inwardly, wishing they would

talk a little more. I knew they preferred to keep the old traditions alive, but I truly cared about them and I wished they felt more comfortable with me.

Then let's fly! And we were off.

Laying spread-eagle in the middle of my meadow buck naked as the setting sun dusted my skin had me relaxing for the first time all day.

You can't possibly be comfortable like that.

"On the contrary, Spirit, I'm more comfortable than I've ever been. This is entirely natural. We're meant to be naked. That's why we shift naked. The first Drakonae shifted naked."

This is why people think you're a weirdo, Esmerelda. You run around naked all the time.

"No, people think I'm a weirdo because I'm the only ice dragon in an entire clan of fire dragons."

Well, that's true, Sprit conceded. ***But I'm sure being naked doesn't help.***

I laughed. "Whatever." I called upon my black dragon scales, manipulating them into a tight bodysuit. "Feel better?"

Yes.

"Speaking of weirdos, why do you think you're so talkative? Most Drakoni aren't like you. I remember when we first bonded. I told my brother and Leo about you and they looked at me like I was strange."

You are strange, Spirit pointed out.

"I'm being serious." I sat up. "I've never heard of another Drakoni being so... outspoken. That's why I named you Spirit."

And we're grateful for you, Esmerelda. I hope you know that. Most Drakonae never even care to name their bonded Drakoni. Of course, we have names, but you could never pronounce them. The ancient language something all Drakoni know from birth, so I don't even know how we'd teach it. I don't know why I am the way I am. Maybe I'm like this so we could find each other? I think you need an extra strong Drakoni. You're special, Esmerelda.

I smiled. Spirit could be snarky, but she was loyal and a fierce protector. "I love you, too." I jumped up and threw my arms around her. Then, I jumped up and ran to my other Drakoni.

"Thank you for your service. I love you guys." I went over to Sun,

Star, and Sky to give them big hugs. They accepted them, albeit reluctantly. However, I could feel their affection for me. *Oh well, not everyone was overly fond of snuggles.*

That's because your body is ice-cold, Esmerelda.

"I can't help that! I'm a damn ice dragon. Ice. Dragon." I huffed. "At least I'm not a frigid bitch like those other ice Drakonae females. That's probably why they don't like me."

We've talked about why they don't like you. It's because you're crazy.

"How so?"

Let's reminisce…

I had a feeling the flashback session wouldn't go well for me, so I started to backtrack. "You know, maybe you're right. I don't think we need to hash this out again."

No, no, you bought it up. Let's do this.

I knew things were about to get quite embarrassing for me when my other Drakoni started snorting in their version of laughter. *Shit.*

Up until you were eight years old, you would run naked everywhere in the clan. You screamed and shifted every time your mother tried to chase you down and tried to put clothes on you.

"I already explained my stance on nakedness. Next." Hm. Not too bad so far.

What about the year you set everything on fire to prove you were, in fact, a fire dragon, not an ice dragon?

"That doesn't sound like me."

That sounds exactly like you.

"Agree to disagree," I muttered.

Okay, fine. How about when you froze all of Chastity's dresses and wardrobe the day before her Debutante Ball, so she had to postpone after she called you "a crazy psycho with no friends" to which you colorfully responded with—and I quote— "Who's the bitch now?"

"No one can prove that was me."

The door was literally frozen shut.

"Still."

You're the only ice dragon in the clan.

"I plead the fifth!" I shouted.

You've ruined at least five potential matches within the first ten minutes of your date.

"Okay, that one is true. But they're truly the worst."

How would you know? You barely talk to them before escaping.

I paused. Well, that was also true. How did I know they were awful? *Because they just are,* I thought tentatively. Obviously. That's a good comeback. I opened my mouth to reply, but Spirit was already looking at me.

I can hear everything you're thinking, and I heard your entire thought process. So, I know that you have no idea if they're actually awful or not.

"Shit, you're right." Maybe I am a crazy.

You are.

"Spirit, come on, you're supposed to be on my side."

I'm on your side, Esmerelda. But you've got some issues.

I squeaked. "Issues! Why don't we talk about your issues next, huh?"

Unfortunately, my tongue-lashing was cut short by the approaching sound of flapping wings. *Saved by the bell, Spirit. We'll hash this out another time.*

Sure, sure.

Five black dragons were closing in on my supposedly private meadow. I wasn't too upset at the interruption, though, because I instantly recognized the one in front as Leo. His wings were on full display and I had a weird urge to shift and lick them all over. I'd chalk that up to my dragon instincts. Definitely not because I was in love with him or whatever bullshit Spirit was spewing.

Okay, weirdo.

"Get out of my head," I muttered.

Can't.

Leo and his Drakoni touched down and he quickly shifted. He, like most Drakonae, didn't enjoy being naked in public. They thought it was *inappropriate*. Prudes, all of them. Unfortunately, that meant that I didn't get the chance to see a lot of skin. Not that I wanted too. Much. Almost in one fluid motion, he had covered his body in a thick scaly armor plating.

"Esme, your mother is looking—" he stopped abruptly as he noticed my outfit. I looked down. It was pretty hot if I did say so myself. And I did. A skin tight body suit, pure obsidian black, like my dragon scales. *What in the Drakoni gods are you wearing?"*

"Oh this? It's a body suit. All the rage on Earth." I smirked.

He crossed his arms. "How would you know that? You've never been there."

"True," I admitted. "But Earth is basically the opposite of here, right? It's our alternate. The other side of our coin. Our double. So, I just assumed that whatever we hate here, they would love. Whatever isn't popular here, would be very stylish there."

"That's an interesting assumption, Esme. How long have you been thinking of this?"

"Quite a while, actually. I used to dream of escaping there. When I was younger and first discovered I was an ice dragon and everyone else in the clan was a fire dragon. I felt like a freak."

"You're not a freak," he said gently.

I looked at him. "Yes, I am. Everyone says so. It's okay, Leo. I've accepted it now. I'm different than everyone else. I don't know why I am the way that I am, and maybe I'll never know. But anyway, I used to imagine that I would runaway to Earth and start a new life where there were no clans, and I didn't have to worry about fitting in. It was nice."

"I didn't know you felt that way."

"Well, I've always tried to hide it. I wanted to be strong for my family. I don't want to seem weak. I'm a Drakonae and Drakonae aren't weak. We're not victims. I'm not a victim." I paused. "Anyway, why are you here? And how did you find me? This is my secret spot."

He laughed. "Esme, I've known that you come here for years. You're not exactly discreet. The opposite of that, really. I just didn't follow you because I know you come here to be alone. I figured you would invite me if you wanted me to come with. But I came here today because your mother is looking for you. You've been gone for hours and it's really late. She's worried about you and so am I. I wanted to check on you."

I blushed. "I'm fine. I guess I just lost track of time. I was just resting, and I might have even fallen asleep for a little bit, honestly." I looked up at him. "Thank you for checking on me. I'm not even mad that you found my secret spot."

He laughed again. "I told you, it wasn't a secret. You're really not discreet at all."

"Fine. I'll try to be sneakier."

He caught my hand. "No, I like knowing where you are." Then, he cleared his throat and pulled away before I could say anything. "Want to fly back together?"

"Hell yes, let's do this." I agreed. "Race you!"

"Please," he scoffed. "You don't have a chance."

"We'll see about that."

Yeah, I lost. But it was still a hell of a good time.

"Esmerelda, are you ready?"

"For what, mother?"

She gasped. Dramatically, again. Was she practicing that in the mirror, or did it just come naturally?

"Gosh, I'm just kidding. Yes, I'm ready for my re-do date with Elias. And don't worry, I'll behave like a good little Drakonae. You and father will be quite proud of me. Where is he anyway? And Lochlan?"

"They're both off on assignment. Don't worry about them. Let me get a look at you." She pulled me closer and examined my face. "You'll do."

"Gee, thanks mom. That's quite the endorsement. I feel beautiful. Truly. You pay me the highest of compliments."

She rolled her eyes. *Damn, she's in quite the mood today.*

Probably because she's worried if you scare this one off, there won't be another.

Hey! I'm a catch.

Sure. Another eye roll. But this time in my head. Damn I was getting destroyed today and it wasn't even lunchtime. It didn't bode well for my upcoming date. *Maybe if it ends early, I can go to my non-secret secret meadow?*

That's one idea that I'll actually stand by, Spirit agreed.

Now that's more like it, I grinned.

A knock came at the door and my mother's eyes widened frantically. "That would be Leo here to pick you up."

"Are you okay?" I asked.

"Yes, I'm fine." She smoothed down her dress. Lady Cassandra Obsidianfire looked more frazzled than I'd ever seen her, and I wondered what was going on with her. Did she have something else riding on this match that I didn't know about? Was this really the last suitor that was courting me? Had I actually scared them all off? Shit. Maybe I was that much of a freak. I sighed as the door opened and Leo stepped inside. I walked up to him and curtsied.

"Shall we, my lady?" he smiled slightly. I held back my laugh because it felt so weird to do the formal escort stuff with Leo, but it was also pretty amusing. We did, however, have to keep up the facade in front of my mother and the rest of my family if they were here. None of them had any idea how close we had gotten in the past couple of years. That he had been training me. It was forbidden. Or at least extremely frowned upon in our society. I hadn't really read the bylaws.

"Of course, Warrior." I took his elbow and we left. He escorted me into the carriage that would take us all the way to the Emeraldice clan and then Elias's estate. It would take a couple hours. Any further and we would have had to fly or leave much earlier and stay the night. Which I *so* did not want to do. Anything to spend as little time as possible with him was what I wanted to do.

"So, round two, huh?" he said.

"Yes," I admitted. "Apparently, he wants a second chance. Although, I don't know why. Maybe because I'm a valuable asset. I guess I am quite an interesting prize to have for another clan. The only ice dragon in a clan of fire dragons."

He contemplated my answer and shook his head. "I don't think that's it."

I looked over at him and raised an eyebrow. "Really? What do you think?"

"I think it's because even though he only spent five minutes in your presence, he could tell how amazing you are. How special you are. How despite growing up as the only ice dragon in a clan of fire dragons, you've been able to become one of the strongest Drakonae I know. Males included. How beautiful you are. I think that he could tell that although you're crazy as hell—" he paused to laugh, "it's because you know what you want, and you go after it with no reservations. And that makes you undeniably imperfectly perfect."

Holy. Shit.

You're right this time, Esmerelda. Holy shit.

Did you just swear, Spirit? I don't think you've ever done that before.

It was totally warranted this time.

"Wow," I said softly. A single tear fell from my left eye. Or was it my right eye? I couldn't tell. Did it matter? *No.* I was freaking out and focusing on the wrong thing. "That's the sweetest thing that anyone has ever said to me before."

"I meant it," he said seriously.

"Would it be weird if I told you that I totally wanted to lick your wings the other day?"

He busted out laughing. "Yes, Esme. That's literally the weirdest thing anyone has ever said to me."

I shrugged. "Well then, I take it back."

"You can't."

"Just did," I insisted.

"Crazy as hell," he muttered. I smiled. We both leaned back and spent the rest of the trip in an amiable silence.

Two hours later, we showed up at the Emeraldice clan. Another ten minutes of driving had us arriving at Elias's estate. I took a deep breath. I really didn't want to do the date. I didn't want to do the first one, and I wanted to do the second even less. Leo had a grim smile on his face which made me think that he felt the same way. But we had no choice.

He jumped out first, gracefully, and held out an arm to help me out. My exit was less graceful, but I made it without falling on my ass. Barely. I looked up to the sky and saw my Drakoni circling above. Their presence made me feel safe and I relaxed at the familiar sight of Spirit's rainbow wings.

Elias was outside before we even got to the door. I raised my eyebrows, unable to hide my surprise.

"Esme, hello, it's so nice to see you again." He leaned over and kissed my hand. The gesture was common and not improper. It was, however, surprising again. I really got the feeling that he didn't like me last time, so I was confused.

He laughed at my obvious confusion. "I see that you're unsure of my intentions. I promise that they're pure. Honestly, I wasn't sure what to expect when I met you. I've met a lot of ice Drakonae females and they're usually quite..." he trailed off, looking for a word.

"Bitchy?"

"Well, yes." He chuckled. "I worried that you might be like that, but I realized that you weren't. I guess it was too late, because I had already run you off. Will you give me a second chance?"

Hm, this is weird. What is happening? Is this a trick?

I don't think so Esmerelda. I think he's being genuine. I don't sense any ill intentions.

What, are you a psychic now?

No. I'm your protector though and he seems like he was just looking out for himself before and lumping you in with the previous bad experiences that he's had. Maybe he'll realize that you're too crazy for him when he gets to know you more, maybe that's something that he'll come to love about you. But you'll never know until you try.

I looked over at Leo who seemed a little queasy.

I thought you said you didn't like him, Spirit taunted.

Ugh, you know that I do. I was totally lying. What am I supposed to do?

I don't know. Just go on this date. You have to, anyway. Your mother will actually murder you if you don't. Spirit had a point. I definitely needed to go on this date no matter if I wanted to or not.

You're right. And who knows if Leo even wants to be with me...

It sure sounded like it earlier.

Yeah, I guess. But he's all noble and stuff and also a Warrior. I'm the only ice dragon in a fire dragon clan and supposed to be married off to another clan to maintain allegiance or whatever. Stupid politics. I sighed. Internally of course. Because the whole conversation was in my head.

Speaking of, it was taking a long time and it probably just looked like I was zoning out. Leo was used to it. Elias, on the other hand, was probably super confused and wondering what the hell was going on with me. He was probably starting to rethink the whole second chance thing. I looked at him, but he was still waiting patiently for me to answer him. Maybe he thought I was just mulling it over in my head. *Sure, we'll go with that.*

"Yes," I finally answered.

"Great! In that case, I have something really fun planned for our date."

"Sounds good to me," I smiled softly.

"Wait here, I'll be right back." Elias ran back inside, leaving Leo and I standing at the door alone.

"So, that was interesting, huh?" I asked as I turned to him.

"Yeah."

"Very surprising. I mean, wow! I never saw that coming."

"Mhm."

"I wonder what we're going to do. It seems we're going someplace else."

"Yeah."

I turned to look at him. Hard face. Flat. Stoic. "Seriously? One-word answers? What's up with that?"

"You had a chance to get out of the date. Why didn't you take it?"

I was starting to get a little angry. "Are you kidding me? That's what this is about? Are you jealous or something?"

"Of course, I'm jealous!"

I paused, surprised. I actually didn't think that he would admit he was jealous. Huh. That was pretty cool. But, back to the real problem.

"Listen, Leo. I'm doing this because I have to. My mother called me an *embarrassment* to the family yesterday. Do you know what that's like? Being the loser of the family? It sucks. She said I need to do this. So even if I wanted to skip out, I can't. And I'm a Drakonae female. Apparently, it's my damn job to get married off to some other clan. No matter what I want. And it doesn't even matter, does it? Because if I left right now and told you that I wanted to be with you, would you accept me? Would you fight for me and be with me? No, you wouldn't. Because you're destined to be married to some other fire dragon, right? And you wouldn't scorn your destiny. Not perfect Leo. So, don't pretend like it matters what I do. Because it doesn't." I angrily wiped my tears and turned away.

Thankfully, Elias returned before I had to endure Leo's response. *Elias with the save.*

I'm proud of you, Esmerelda. You stood up for yourself.

Thanks, Spirit. It felt good. A little soul-crushing, but good.

"So, Elias, where are we going?"

He smiled widely. "The Crystal Mountains." *Oh, hell yes!*

As it turns out, Elias was not terrible. He was actually quite pleasant. I really enjoyed his company. Did I want to lick his wings? No. So I didn't think we would be a good match. But he would make a fantastic best friend. However, I decided to hold off telling him that until we finished our date because I really wanted to go to the Crystal Mountains.

The Crystal Mountains was the Drakoni homeland. It was where all of the unbonded Drakoni lived and were young Drakonae went to find Drakoni to bond with. They were gorgeous; luminescent and made entirely of gemstones. The mountain range was all over Drakon and Emeraldice was near a good climbing spot, so we didn't have to travel far. It would obviously be quicker to shift and fly, but we decided to hike so it would be easier to talk. It was also a beautiful day for hiking.

"We're almost to the top!" Elias shouted.

"Yay!" I yelled back. "I'm so excited. This really is the best date ever. Truly, such a good idea."

He laughed. "It's probably the best date ever because it's the longest. How many guys did you scare off before me? And how long did they even last?"

I grinned. "Okay, that may be true. Let's see. You're the fifth. First one was one hour. Second was forty-five minutes. The third one made it thirty minutes. I thought I had it down to a pattern by then. But then the fourth made it twenty. And then there was you. I scared you off in five minutes. Best record by far."

"Ah, yes. But I came back."

"That's also true," I admitted. "No one ever did that. Something *must* be wrong with you."

He laughed. "Or something is wrong with everyone before me."

I smiled. "I like that explanation much better."

We finally reached the top. Leo walked up a about thirty seconds later. He had maintained a respectable distance, as required by an escort. He was being quite broody, if I did say so myself. And I so did.

"Damn, this is gorgeous," I whispered.

"It is," Elias agreed.

Even Leo nodded. I felt Spirit's happiness in my head, along with that of my other Drakoni. They hadn't been back to the Crystal Mountains in years. I resolved to go back more often so they could feel closer to their Drakoni ancestors.

Thank you, Esmerelda. That's more than we would ever ask of you.

I'd do anything for you.

"Do you want to go inside? I think there's an opening up there." Elias looked at me. Heck yes, I wanted to go inside.

Spirit, would that be okay?

Of course, Esmerelda.

I felt her burning desire to go inside as well and made a snap decision. *You should come, too.*

It's too small. I won't fit.

Shift into your smaller form, I suggested.

Seconds later, a small dragon with rainbow wings flew over and touched down on my shoulder.

Elias raised an eyebrow.

"She wants to go, too," I explained.

"So, we're going?" he asked excitedly.

"Hell yes, we're going."

"Then let's do this."

"Race you!" I called out as I took off toward the opening. He laughed and chased me. Leo sighed and ran after us. I won. Did they let me win? Probably. Did I care? Hmm, not really.

"Okay, so here we are. Now what?" I asked.

"Well, let's just go inside and explore," Elias said.

"Sure. I haven't been here since I bonded with my Drakoni. It's been so long. Like twenty years."

"I went once when my Drakoni was sick. I was fifteen. We went down to the deep parts of the Crystal Mountains. Tried to find some of the really ancient Drakoni and get some answers. They know things. Things we don't remember. About bloodlines, medicine, and the beginning of both our species." Elias said.

I gasped. Shit, was I turning into my mother? "Wow, did you find the answers you were looking for?"

"Well, my Drakoni did. I couldn't see or hear the ancient Drakoni. But we must have managed to get deep enough that he heard something. He told me that he had the answer, and he was ready to leave. So, I took him back up and he was better in a few days. I haven't been back since then. Until today. I thought you would want to come. I had a feeling you might want some answers for yourself."

I was both intrigued and touched. I did want answers. Why was I this way? The only ice dragon in a clan of fire dragons? And I knew that Spirit probably wanted some answers for herself. Why was she so different from all other Drakoni? How could I get answers though? Elias said that he couldn't even see them, let alone talk to them.

I felt Spirit buzzing in my head. ***I think you're different Esmerelda. They'll talk to you. They will sense that you're different, I know it.***

Maybe. Either way, we'll find out soon enough.

"Thank you, Elias. That's very kind of you. I do have some answers that I've been looking for." I gave him an impulsive hug and he tightened his arms around me. "You've been quite unexpected."

"Of course, Esme."

Out of the corner of my eye, Leo looked pissed and sad. I didn't even think it was possible to combine those two emotions into one facial expression, but apparently, he could.

I cleared my throat. "Shall we?"

"We shall," Elias smiled. He guided me through the cavern and down through the deepest part of the Crystal Mountains. The closer we got to where the ancient Drakoni rested, the more I started to feel... something. Spirit began feeling a little restless as well.

We're getting close.

I know, I can tell. I feel it, I told her. *I think we need to be alone when we go in though. They won't see us if we're not alone.*

I agree.

How do we get rid of our companions? Stage a coup? Run away naked? Naked distraction? Naked—

Why does literally everything have to do with being naked?

I shrugged. *That's how I do.*

You're a weirdo.

Am not. Like I said, being naked is natural.

We do not have time to argue about nakedness again. Spirit sighed. ***Just ask to go in alone. They will understand. It's a personal question. Damn, you're crazy.***

Oh, that works too.

"Hey, Elias. Leo." They both turned at the sounds of their names. "Do you mind if I go on alone at the end? I want to ask my question and try to get some answers with Spirit as my guide, but I feel like it's kind of a personal thing and I should do it on my own."

Elias raised an eyebrow again at my mention of my Drakoni's name. Shit, I forgot that I hadn't said it before in front of him. *Whoops.*

"Of course, Esme. I understand. I'll just wait here. Call out if you need anything." Elias smiled at me and I curtsied back. He grinned and shook his head a bit because he knew by know that I was not the curtseying type.

I turned toward Leo, but he remained stoic. His face was hard as stone and his arms were crossed. I tried to mimic his stance, but I wasn't very intimidating. My pale skin, long black hair, turquoise eyes, bejeweled face, and pastel yellow dress didn't exactly say "scary."

"Leo—er, Warrior Leo, please." I begged.

"I don't really feel comfortable letting you go in alone."

"Please, I won't be gone long, I swear."

He paused. Elias looked back and forth between us, examining our stances, our faces, and our words. I wondered what he saw and what he was thinking.

"Fine." Leo sighed. "But if you're not out in twenty minutes, I'm coming in after you."

"Of course. Perfectly reasonable response," I nodded.

He shot me a look. I straightened and smiled. "Twenty minutes, I got it!"

"Good. Be safe."

"Always am."

"Yeah, sure," he muttered.

I curtsied again at both of them, straightened up, and saluted.

"Farewell, my lords, I will return in a scant twenty minutes. Don't miss me too much!" I blew them a kiss before I left and winked. Elias caught it—very smooth of him—and Leo rolled his eyes.

Once I was out of sight, I sprinted, following my gut and Spirit's instructions to the deepest part of the mountains where the ancient Drakoni would be. It took about five minutes until we felt like we were at the right place. I stopped and looked around. It looked similar to the place I was at with Leo and Elias, but it was different, too. It was cozier. It was darker because it was deeper in the mountains, but it was lighter because there were more gemstones and they glowed brighter. Overall, the effect was gorgeous. I felt Spirit's awe inside my head.

Wow.

"Wow is right, Spirit. This is amazing. I can't believe that we're here. I wish we could spend more time. I wish you could spend more time here. I'm sorry that we haven't been back before this. I promise we will go more often. You deserve it. This is where you're meant to be. This is your birthright."

SPIRIT, AS YOU CALL HER, IS RIGHT. YOU'RE DIFFERENT FROM THE REST, ESMERELDA OBSIDIANFIRE. OR SHOULD WE EVEN CALL YOU OBSIDIANFIRE? IT'S OBVIOUS THAT YOU'RE AN ICE DRAGON. The voice came from all around me and I'd never heard anything like it before. There was an enormous dragon hidden deep in the shadows mostly out of sight, only flecks of red peeking through the darkness.

"Holy shit!" I covered my mouth. How embarrassing. I just swore in front of an ancient Drakoni. "I'm very sorry, Ancient One. Or should I call you something else? Do you have a name?"

The male Drakoni chuckled. *NONE THAT YOU CAN PRO-NOUNCE, YOUNG DRAKONAE. YOU CAN, HOWEVER, GIVE ME ONE IF YOU'D LIKE. OR YOU CAN CONTINUE CALLING ME ANCIENT ONE. WHATEVER YOU PREFER.*

"What do your wings look like?"

INTERESTING QUESTION. He paused. *MY WINGS ARE BRIGHT RED.*

"Okay, I'll call you Crim. Short for Crimson."

I LIKE IT. SO, ESMERELDA, WHY HAVE YOU COME TO THE CRYSTAL MOUNTAINS TODAY?

"Well, that's a long story, but I've come down here to talk to you because I wanted to ask you a question."

I SEE. WHAT IS IT YOU WISH TO KNOW?

"Who am I? Why am I the way I am? An ice dragon in a fire dragon clan, I mean?"

HM. Crim paused. *LET ME SEE. WOULD YOU MIND IF I TOOK A SNIFF OF YOUR BLOOD?*

"Have at it!" I held out my arm and Crim shuffled over. He swiped a dragon claw gently against my arm.

He chuckled again. *YOU ARE AMUSING, YOUNG DRAKONAE.*

"Thank you. Everyone else just thinks I'm crazy."

She is crazy, Spirit blurted.

I shot her the evil eye but kept a sweet smile on my face.

"Hush, now, Spirit. There's no need to be telling Crim all these lies about me."

THE TRUTH OF YOUR BLOODLINES LIES WITHIN YOU. YOU ARE NOT A FREAK OF NATURE, AS SOME MIGHT HAVE YOU BELIEVE. MORE LIKE A GENETIC MIRACLE GOING BACK TO ANCIENT TIMES.

My eyes widened at Crim's analysis of my blood. "How so?"

YOUR BLOOD SHOWS THAT YOU ARE OF MY BLOODLINE.

"Wow! That's so cool. Like how far down the line? You must have an ice dragon in there somewhere I guess, right?"

YES, WE DO. MY MATE, ACTUALLY.

My mouth dropped open. Holy shit. It was extremely rare for dragons of opposite powers to mate with each other. Especially ancient ones. Practically unheard of.

"How is it possible that I'm an ice dragon if I'm so far down the line?"

THAT IS THE WEIRD PART. THE WAY YOUR BLOOD SMELLS… IT SEEMS LIKE YOU ARE MUCH, MUCH CLOSER IN THE BLOODLINE.

"Like how close?"

CLOSE ENOUGH THAT YOU COULD BE MY DAUGHTER.

Holy. Shit.

"Well damn. I wasn't expecting that."

NOR WAS I, YOUNG DRAKONAE.

"I'll have to think on this, Crim. Maybe ask my parents some questions. Thank you for answering. I appreciate it. Do you have time to answer something for Spirit as well?"

OF COURSE.

Thank you, Ancient One.

PLEASE, SPIRIT, CALL ME CRIM.

Sprit looked surprised but inclined her head.

Okay, Crim. I wanted to ask a similar question as Esmerelda, but about myself. What makes me different?

I WILL PERFORM THE SAME TEST. Crim walked over to Spirit and took a swipe of her blood. He sniffed it and immediately straightened up, eyes wide. *YOU ARE CLOSE TO THE CHANGE.*

Spirit's eyes almost bulged out of her little dragon head.

"What does that mean?" I asked.

Apparently, Crim and Spirit decided that I didn't deserve an answer because they started staring at each other and conversing in silence—freaking assholes—while I was pacing around and wondering what in the *hell* was going on.

"What does that mean!" My eyes widened in horror, probably also looking like they were going to pop out of my head. "Oh, my Drakoni gods, are you going to change into a frog? That would be awful. I hate frogs."

What are you talking about, Esmerelda? Just relax, I'm not going to turn into a frog.

Whew. That was close.

No, it wasn't. There was literally no chance that I was going to turn into a frog.

I shrugged. *We'll talk about this later*, I said to her.

"Crim, thank you for everything. We need to go though, because I have two *boys* who are going to freak out and come after me if I'm not back in like six minutes. Can we come visit again?"

OF COURSE, ESMERELDA. SPIRIT. IT WAS A PLEASURE TO MEET YOU BOTH. I HOPE TO SEE YOU SOON.

I curtsied and then sprinted out, running as fast as I could so I made the twenty-minute deadline. I was probably cutting it very close. There was a 98% chance that Leo was already coming after me, but there was important stuff going on that I couldn't have just walked out on, so I was fine if he was upset with me for a little while. It was worth it. I finally had some answers. Although, I also had more questions. Like why was my bloodline so weird? And *what the hell was Spirit changing into?* Was she going to leave me?

I'll never leave you, Esmerelda.

You say that now, but you can't know for sure, Spirit.

Not true. I know what's in my heart.

"Esme! Esme! Are you okay?" Leo ran up and grabbed my arm which—shit—had some dried blood on it.

"Oh, I'm totally fine. I just scratched it while I was running back. I didn't think I would make the deadline, and I totally just ran right into the wall. Clumsy of me. How embarrassing. It doesn't hurt, I swear."

Elias came over with a first aid kit and bandaged it up. Very handy of him. "All better."

"See, Leo? Good as new!"

He sighed. "I knew we shouldn't have let you go off alone."

"I'm fine. Really. It's not a big deal," I insisted.

He looked unconvinced. I poked it. "Look: straight face. Didn't even flinch." Finally, he cracked a smile. I turned to Elias.

"Elias, thank you so much for the suggestion. It was amazing. I can't believe that I haven't been down here before."

"So, did you find what you were looking for?" he asked.

"Maybe. It was a start at least." I smiled.

"Good. I'm glad."

"Me too." I smiled again. "Let's head back. I'm starving."

Elias laughed. "Absolutely. Now that I remember, I think I do owe you lunch."

"How was the date?"

"It was actually really fun, mother. Thank you for insisting I give Elias a second chance."

Lady Cassandra looked extremely smug. And yes, she should be because I did like Elias. But the real reason that I was very grateful for her insistence was, of course, the trip to the Crystal Mountains.

"I'm very happy to hear that, Esmerelda."

"Now if you don't mind, mother, I am going flying for a bit to clear my mind."

"Not at all. Have a good flight." I kissed her on the cheek and walked outside. I ran to the clearing where I always shifted, disrobed, and changed into dragon form. My Drakoni met me in the sky. We flew quickly to my non-secret secret meadow. I had a lot to think about.

When I landed, I shifted back and put on my armored body suit, so Spirit felt comfortable. She landed softly beside me.

"So, not a freak of nature, huh?" I laughed. "That's a relief. If only I could go back in time and tell all those bullies."

That would really show them.

"You're totally right, Spirit. As usual. The bloodline thing is so weird though, right? What's that about?"

No idea. We'll have to look into it more, I guess. Do more research, maybe?

"Knock some heads? Naked stuff?"

No, like normal research. In a library.

"That doesn't sound fun," I pouted.

It never is.

I turned to her. "Will you tell me what the Change is now?"

You really don't know?

"No, I don't."

C'mon, Esmerelda. Think about it. What do you think it is?

I thought. I really took the time to think about it. And suddenly it came to me. And I felt like a freaking idiot for thinking that Spirit was going to turn into a frog. In my defense, I was in a weird state of mind.

"Holy shit. It isn't—are you—uhm—"

Yes. I'm going to shift.

"Holy. Shit."

***

Read more about Drakonae and Drakoni in Obsidianfire (The Adventures of Ruby Cross) *featuring Esme's brother, Lochlan! These characters will also make an appearance.*

ND Gray is afraid of heights and would make a terrible dragon rider. No one likes a screaming, hysterical, backseat driver who pushes the imaginary break All. The. Time. But a tiny horde of tiny dragons? Yes please! And her main character agrees, even though it means one must make strange fashion choices. The pay off is: when things go wrong, the horde will stampede to the rescue. (With dreams of charcoal biskies dancing in their heads.)

WHAT WE LEAVE BEHIND

ND Gray

IT WAS A HOTEL ROOM filled with the echoes of tears and the taste of despair. On this particular day, it was also haunted by a specter of old anger.

The ancient carpeting had once been designed to look like autumn leaves scattered on the ground. Over the years, the passing of many feet had turned the carpet pattern into a worn, muddy-orange field with random and unsightly stains. There had once been a flood, if not of water, then of some other fluid. It had seeped through the thin pile and bled the color out of the crushed leaves.

On one of the room's two beds, the thin russet covers were twisted to the side revealing an off-white sheet and an old pillow dented by the many heads that had lain upon it. Weak morning light slanted through the half-opened dusty blinds. It lay in stripes across the fluid-stained floor, and the crinkled sheets of the used-up bed, and the still, small person on the far bed, which half-blocked the bathroom door. The door stood ajar and had a crack running up and down it. From the darkness behind it, a faucet dripped steadily.

On the grimy, beige walls above the beds, uninspired prints of dead trees against pale winter skies clung to thin nails. One print was slipping out of its cheap plastic frame and another hung at a crooked slant. Flashes of blue light shone randomly off of its thin glass as images flickered on the old, brown TV set.

A knob had broken off the set long ago, leaving the sound stuck just below comfortable hearing.

A ratty chair—the sort one finds in hotel rooms such as this— the sort with a badly upholstered, tan and rust-colored cushion and a large uncomfortable gap in the back—had been placed at an angle before the screen. The chair creaked as the man sitting in it leaned forward and turned the knob to change the channel.

SULLY WAS MISSING.

Mrs. Amelia St. George didn't want to admit it, but she was worried. The jerky snack in his bowl had not been touched. The lighter fluid in his dish was as full as it had been when she'd topped it off last evening. His favorite perch, empty; his favorite chew toy — the small, metal knight in fairly dented, tooth-marked armor – was upside down near the fireplace.

Mrs. St. G had been to the park an hour before, as Sully often wandered over there to hunt dragonflies at the pond. In the house, she had searched through every room. The kitchen. Pantry. Formal parlor. Informal parlor. Dining room and Conservatory.

Then, upstairs. The bedrooms and the library. The linen cupboards and the laundry and the room of small gewgaws.

She had traipsed down to the basement. Its cement floor was polished, and the block walls whitewashed. The area at the bottom of the stairs was nice and tidy with a counter, table, and sink. A few old cupboards held ointments, salves, crushed & jarred herbal remedies. A well-worn leather satchel held a small surgical kit. It sat on a rolling table and the shelves beneath it were piled with first aid tape, bandages, and a large plastic container of Q-tips.

Beyond this space, the basement became a warren of narrow passageways lined by block-walled cul-de-sacs bursting with a century's worth, or more, of the accumulated treasures of life. It was as if several flea markets had come here to retire. Somewhere in the chaos, Mrs. St. G's wedding dress hung beside her great grandmother's bee keeping costume and her great, great-grand-father's everyday sword.

His ceremonial sword was displayed on the mantel in the library. The rubies in handle would glitter in the rays slanting rough the tall windows with the stained-glass insets at the top. A ruby and gold handled sword was not the strangest thing in Mrs. St. G's house.

It was an old house. The houses in the surrounding neighborhood were all mouthy, young, upstarts by comparison. The town's many files of building blueprints and building permits had not a single record of the house because it had been built long before there was a town.

It was an odd house. For one thing, all the pictures were hung in a single row at the very top of the walls. They weren't simply hung, they were bolted in. The wallpaper was old, the silver and sapphire feather pattern faded into a sort of gray. Along the bottom of these gray walls, for a height of two feet or so, were thousands of scratch marks, as if a very short person had walked around with a letter opener in their hand, dragging the tip across the wall. In time, mere scratches had turned into groves.

The furniture in the house was covered by the most hideous coverings. Only the color and patterns on the drapes were uglier. Neither covering nor drapes had not been chosen for their aesthetic appeal but for their flame retarding capabilities.

Here and there, the walls had singe marks, as if someone had sneezed and their sneezes had flashed fire for a brief second. The singe marks explained the glass case bolted over the large portrait hanging on the parlor wall. A man and a woman, he with white hair, she with short curls the color of blue-gray steel. They stood side by side. The artist had captured the harmony of the couple's body language--holding hands and leaning slightly toward each other, even though their focus was somewhere behind the painter's shoulder. Like many couples who have aged together through the long, topsy-turvy years of life, they looked like each other. Similar smiles. Similar glints in their bespectacled eyes. A fountain pen had been tucked behind his ear; a small ink splot seeped into the shoulder of his cream shirt. She wore a pale blue blouse with small summer roses printed on it. They both wore baggy firefighter pants and thick boots.

A decade older, but dressed almost the same way as in the portrait—her blouse had a pink rose print today—Mrs. St. G experienced a rare moment of melancholy. What would happen to all her treasures, all this history, when she was gone? What would happen to Sully and the strays. And the others away out back in the deep woods?

She had nearly a dozen nieces and nephews, but none had the Sight.

There was the Ferguson boy, but he was young. He wouldn't enjoy visiting one doddering old woman and her strays for much longer. Puberty would hit. His schedule would fill up. High school. College. He would manage to convince himself his memories were overlain with dreams.

Someday, out and about in his adult life, he might see a stray. He might have a moment of clarity. Of Sight. He might come back to seek the answers to questions tumbling through his mind.

Would she live long enough for that to happen?

Sighing, she walked away from the visual cacophony of the retired flea markets and up through her sprawling house. Walked slowly to the spiral stair leading around and around, up to the spired turret at the very top of the house where the late Mr. St. G had used his beautiful telescope to chart the stars.

His notes and constellation diagrams were tacked to the walls, and books about space, the universe, and all things cosmic were stacked on the floor, window seat, and what little shelf space existed in the turret.

She didn't come up here much these days. There was a lot of dust. But no Sully. After a moment of remembering Frank, head tilted as he peered into the telescope, she left the turret, shutting the door quietly behind her.

She had just returned to the ground floor when someone rang the doorbell.

OFFICER MINERVA GREAVES DEPRESSED THE brake pedal as they approached the next driveway, and the next house on the list. Here on Cave Street (which was a strange name for the street as there were no caves for miles and miles around) the estates were spaced out too far to make walking door to door via the long and winding sidewalk convenient. Especially for police officers on a matter of great urgency.

Slowing the cruiser, Officer Greaves tuned into the drive of number seventy-three, the lawns of which had been bordered by tall, neatly trimmed hedges. The spired turret on the top-most floor of the house could be seen above the hedge, so she had been prepared for the remainder of the sprawling house. Its midnight blue paint, and gold and silver trim which feature elegant starbursts, was unusual, but not shocking. The lawns on the other hand....

In the passenger seat, her partner, Officer Wilson Todd, gave a grunt of surprise. Greaves drove very slowly up the long, sloping drive as she and her partner stared out of the windows at the lawns covered in random mounds of dirt. Some of the dirt piles were large, taller than the police cruiser. Others were small, like the disturbed soil around a gopher hole. Some appeared to have small caves dug into and beneath them, little earthen hidey-holes. More than a few of these cavelettes had the odds and ends of life stashed in them. Squashed soda cans, a deflated beach ball, a pink pedal from a bicycle.

The officers exited their cruiser—Greaves pulling her hat firmly over her tight curls and Todd hitching up his uniform pants, settling it into place over his ever-expanding belly. She was younger than he. His skin was pasty, hers rich brown. He was shorter, she leaner. But both wore the same expression of wary curiosity as Greaves rang the bell.

From somewhere inside the house a deep, sonorous tone rolled out, as if a bell as large as the house itself had been struck. And then smaller, brighter bell tones rang out over the still resounding deep note. A playful, fluid melody that neither officer recognized. Still, some place inside them understood that even though they had never heard it before, they had always known this song.

The heavy front door, carved with a blazing, golden-starburst swung slowly inward on silent hinges, and a petite woman with short, steel-gray curls smiled up at them, her eyes twinkling over half-moon spectacles. Despite the twinkle, there was something fierce in those eyes, in the set of the slim shoulders, "Hello, Officers. How may I help you?"

It took a moment for Greaves to register that the woman had spoken to them. And another moment to gather her thoughts, as her attention was quite taken with the older woman's appearance. The flower-printed blouse was lovely. The diamond brooch of a star, stunning—though questionable for everyday wear. It was, however, the baggy fire fighter's pants and thickly soled boots that Greaves could not get past.

"We're Officers Greaves and Todd," Todd mumbled in a dazed tone of voice. "She's Todd. I'm Greaves –"

"*I'm* Greaves," the real Greaves cut in. "Do you live here, ma'am?"

"I do," the old woman said, stepping out to join the officers on the wide front porch. "Mrs. Amelia St. George at your service."

Greaves thought that an odd statement, but if she was going to quibble about oddities, they'd be here all day. "Mrs. St. George, do you know the Fergusons from down the street?"

"Aye," the woman nodded firmly. "Why is it that you're askin'?"

"What can you tell me about them?" Greaves pitched her voice to sound almost bored and Todd, thumbs hooked into his belt, studied the pattern of colored glass at the top of a nearby window as if he didn't care about the answer.

The small woman tilted her head. "He's a businessman. Owns a car lot or two. She's a councilwoman. You'd know that better than I."

"And what can you tell us about their son?" For good measure, Greaves threw a barely concealed but completely fabricated yawn into the question. A non-verbal "Nothing to see here." Just a couple of officers asking routine questions about nothing in particular.

The twinkle went out of the eyes and the fierceness sharpened. "Young Topher? What's happened?"

"We do not know that anything has happened. Does he ever trespass on your property?" Greaves eyed the lawn, betting that the caves with their odd stashes of shiny refuse were a hazard to anyone walking across the thick, rich green grass. And more than one mound of dirt could easily conceal a boy of Topher's size. She returned her attention—sharper, less amused—to the petite, older woman.

"He does not trespass on my property." The words were said firmly.

Todd nodded as if he understood the importance of the words. "Trespass is a strong word. Does he ever drop by? Perhaps to ring your bell and dash away? Or look through the... er, piles of... um, treasure?"

"No." The old woman sent a look over her half-moon spectacles like the thrust of a saber.

Greaves tried a different tact. "When would you say was the last time you saw him?"

"Yesterday afternoon," the older woman answered immediately. "He brought me flowers from his mother's garden."

"He does that often?" Todd asked.

"Sometimes. His own grandmother's visit seldom and his parents keep him on a tight leash. Not to speak ill of the job they're doing in raising him. But, I believe... Well, he's always very polite, is young Topher. But sad, like."

"When he came to deliver the flowers, how long would you say he was here?" Greaves asked. Her voice was no longer bored, but it was not overly eager, though she felt her pulse pick up. Finally, they might have a lead.

"Twenty minutes, give or take. We put the flowers in a vase. I offered him a cookie and a glass of milk. He left soon after. Music lesson, I believe."

Greaves caught herself nodding and stopped.

" What has happened to Young Topher?" The woman looked between the two officers, her jaw set firmly.

"You'll appreciate that we are not at liberty to say." Greaves liked this statement. She had learned from one of the department's detectives. What a fancy way to say, "Mind your own business."

"Mmmm," The older woman narrowed her eyes.

"Would you care if we had a look around?" Greaves waved her hand as if to indicate the odd yard and the tree line beyond that.

"Yes. I do mind."

Todd cleared his throat and dropped his voice to a soft baritone with a bit of an "aw, shucks, I'm tubby, nearly-retired, and perfectly harmless" twang thrown in. "Do you know how that's going to look on our report, ma'am? Your refusal to let us look around?"

Slim shoulders squared and set. " I do. But I have nothing to hide and too many gewgaws to be broken if strangers go traipsing through my house."

IN THE DISMAL HOTEL ROOM, the young boy on the bed was frightened and confused. He didn't understand why the man in the creaky chair in front of the TV had done this. Why shove him into that old, beat up van with the dented sliding door? Why tie his hands up and wrap duct tape around his ankles and shove an old sock in his mouth?

The sock tasted like fuzz and feet. Beside the feeling of betrayal, the sock was the worst part of all of this. Of something that had to be a joke. Maybe the man turning the knob on the television, flicking through channels almost too fast to really see anything, was playing a prank. That was it. The man, who was now cleaning his fingernails with the tip of a large knife, was pranking the boy's father. Relived, the boy sighed through the musty sock.

In the big, buttoned-up, side pocket of the boy's pants, something moved. It tented the fabric. The boy winced as little, sharp talons briefly pushed through the khaki material and into his leg. Then the creature's claws were retracted as he settled into a new position with a soft snort. A moment later, the creature had fallen into a deep sleep.

Sometime after that, the man shut off the TV with an angry growl. "Nothing!"

The chair creaked as the man stood, his face in shadow. "We'll have to be... creative."

He walked toward the bed and the boy laying on it.

The boy felt his heart pound as the weak light shone dully on the blade of the knife in his uncle's hand.

Mrs. St. G stood by the kitchen door and removed a heavy key from a hook on the wall. It was an old key. The kind they didn't make any more. As was the padlock to which it belonged. She pushed open the screen door, hoping Sully would be in the backyard with the strays.

As it opened, the door's spring stretched with a metallic twang. The early afternoon breeze immediately stirred the neatly arranged curls laying across the nape of her neck and around her ears. It brought the scent of freshly turned earth and hot rocks.

The porch floor creaked as she stepped outside. She held onto the screen door until it was mostly closed. Then, the spring pulled it the rest of the way shut with a solid, wooden thump. As soon as the door *thumped*, the horde of strays swarmed up from yard. Honking, snorting, growling, and roaring in squeaky little ways, they clustered around her legs. Their scales made a soft rasping noise against the canvas of her firefighter pants. Despite her best attempts to take in the waistband and hem the legs, she practically swam in the danged things. But baggy pants were preferable to toasted legs.

"Easy now, Frank," Mrs. St. G said, holding onto a nearby rocking chair as a particularly large, goldenrod yellow stray bumped against her knees.

She'd named the dragon Frank after her late husband because both of them had terrible allergies, could stare at the stars for hours, and had farts which would burn the hairs right out of one's nostrils before lodging in the sinus cavities for a day or two.

Careful to avoid the four sharp horns, she scratched Frank behind his floppy, trumpet shaped ears, then held out her hand for teeny, brightly-colored Flit. The wings of the palm-sized dragon beat with a shurring sound as she delicately wrapped one claw around Mrs. St. G's thumb. Strings of fire fluid drooped from the little dragon's mouth, but, poor dear, she hadn't flamed yet.

"All in good time," Mrs, St. G said as she settled Flit onto a semi-charred railing before turning her attention to the chain-wrapped, chest freezer in the corner of the porch.

It was a white freezer but covered with so many claw marks, it looked gray. The lid had many bite marks, too. All along the edges, especially the corners, which were partially gnawed away.

The chest was wrapped in an old iron chain as thick as Mrs. St. G's wrist, but that didn't seem to faze the petite, elderly lady as she inserted the key into the dinner-plate-sized padlock holding the chains together. Just before she turned the key, flashing lights caught her eye. Squinting, she peered down across the lawns, through the bordering trees, across the corner of the park, to the curve in the road.

She could just make out that the lights turned in at the Ferguson's. Certain this had something to do with that bright, young boy, Topher, she shooed the dragons away from her legs and made her way back into the house.

With a clatter of claws and disgruntled growls and hisses at the delay of dinner, the strays followed. The screen door was pulled out of Mrs. St. G.'s hand as the little horde bunched up, pushing wing and snout and claw forward to squeeze through the doorway in one writhing mass. The colorful mass bulged as the slimmer dragons attempted to slide over, under, or between the larger dragons. Those few blessed the ability of flight, darted over the roiling horde with no small sense of self-satisfaction and superiority.

"Mind your manners," Mrs St, G said as the last of the group burst into the kitchen, the screen door slamming shut and narrowly missing a blue tail.

Claws clicking on the tiled floor, the bulk of the horde followed close behind their benefactor. Some ran over to snatch up the jerky from Tully's dish, drank from his bowl of lighter fluid, and examined his kitchen perch.

Others darted under the table, long tongues flicking out to lick up the few crumbs that could be found. Others went straight to the source, leaping, climbing, or flying to the stone counter tops. Long reptilian snouts and tongues investigated every nook and cranny, searching for a little munchy. One sleek and sinuous dragon with a mane of shockingly bright vermillion feathers hooked his front claws through the handles of the metal cupboard. Bracing his rear legs on the cupboard bottom, he strained to open the cupboard door behind which he knew were cans of tuna and sardines.

Sardines......

His tongue danced in the air as he redoubled his efforts to rattle open the door. But the dreaded Chain of Prohibition padlocked over the bronze-shaded steel door thwarted his efforts.

"Away from the cupboards, Alfonse," Mrs St. G said without looking as she climbed the backstairs leading out of the far end of the kitchen and up to the second and third floors. Sighing so hard is lips vibrated, Alfonse dropped down to the polished stone counter and then onto the floor, head drooping for a moment before he scrambled after the horde.

Some of the strays could easily hop up the steps. Others shifted onto hind legs and stretched up to grasp the next step with their talons. Back legs scrambling, they clawed their way upward. Some used the spindles of the railing to shimmy up, or the railing itself. Alfonse by passed them all by leaping onto the wall itself. Claws sinking into the plaster, he "ran" above the heads of his hordemates.

Mrs. St. G went up to the third floor, to one of the western rooms where Franklin had stored old astronomy digests, extra telescopes and telescope pieces, and the space rocks that didn't make it into the collection in the turret. Replicas of the planets hung from the ceiling and she threaded her way through Jupiter and Mars as she went to the window.

A handy, handheld telescope rested in its cradle on a nearby shelf, leftover from when Franklin enjoyed scanning for birds in the Park beyond the boarder of trees. There was a list tacked to the wall. The names of birds printed on it in Frank's neat lettering. Beneath his list, *Checkered Blue Finch* was inked in her own angled scrawl.

The park was technically part of the St. George estate, but as the town had grown up, they had created the park for the community and as an insurance policy that they'd never have other houses built close to their own. The park stretched several miles west and three times as many north, curving back along the St. George estate which was thick with woods interspersed with meadows and gurgling streams.

Somewhere back in the woods was a lovely lake, a cousin to the pond in the park where children caught frogs and fishermen tried their luck and joggers followed the surrounding trail, trying to ignore the twinges in their knees and the dogs giving chase. Mrs. St. G turned the handy telescope onto the front corner of her lawn, and then up across the street, across the Ferguson's hedges, to the news vans and police cars filling their wide, circular drive.

"What in the shining scales…," she said, slowly lowering the telescope. But she knew. In her bones, she knew. She'd lived a good long while—still not as old as she would get, but closer to "as old as" than to "as young as".

She returned the telescope to its cradle and stared out over the park without really seeing it. Without seeing the picnic shelter where she'd looked for Sully early in the morning. He often wondered into park looking for treasures to drag home. He—

A memory flashed into her mind. Topher had fed Sully part of a cookie and Sully had sat on his shoulder until Topher was ready to leave. That was the last time she'd seen the little dragon. And probably the last time Topher had been seen as well.

Somewhere between the safety of her home and the safety of his one, someone had taken that bright young boy.

Someone...

Another memory thrust its way to the forefront of her thoughts, clarifying and terrifying. A fierce look washed over her face. The horde of strays scattered as they caught the change in her energy.

Scattered swiftly and silently as she turned and stalked out of the door.

It is said that little old ladies with nothing to lose are fearless. None of them could ever hold a candle to Mrs. St. G's fearlessness. It was a flamethrower.

TOPHER FERGUSON'S HAND ACHED. A drumming sensation pounded through it where it rested on the sheets. Several wadded-up socks had been duct taped over the place where his little finger had been.

His tears had long since dried up. The gross sock in his mouth was soaked through with the tears that had run down the inside of his nose and throat, pooling in his mouth until he swallowed them down.

At least Sully hadn't woken up.

Topher had tried to stay quiet so the little dragon wouldn't come to investigate. He didn't know if his uncle could see dragons—not everyone could, Mrs. St. G said—but the boy felt it would be very bad for the dragon if his uncle spotted him. So Topher sniffled quietly and bravely, silently hoping Sully remained sleeping.

To keep his mind off how much his hand hurt, Topher watched the channels as his uncle flipped through them. Until–

His uncle stopped changing the channels as a woman's face filled the screen. Her brown cheeks were streaked with fresh tears.

Topher's heart clenched and he almost choked as he gasped, drawing in tears and saliva. Someone was asking her a question.

A male speaker was saying, " ...Has it been confirmed?"

The crying woman stood ramrod straight. Despite the tears,

she looked all business in a navy blue suit, her black hair pulled into an elegant twist. She cleared her throat while blinking rapidly. "Yes. It is my son's finger."

"Councilwoman, why was your son's finger sent to Channel Nine?"

"Do you know who might have done this to your child?"

"What are the police doing to find your son?"

The questions were shouted out all at once and the camera view pulled back to show a crowd of reporters before the woman who was, herself, standing in front of the white pillared porch of her brick home.

A man, shorter than the woman, with bright red hair much like Topher's own, stepped forward to place his arm around his wife's waist. He leaned forward. "We'll let the chief answer the procedural questions, but we have no enemies. No one we know would do this. I am offering a substantial reward to anyone who passes along information useful in finding our son. Chief?"

He turned toward the shortest man present while at the same time tugging his wife away from the podium. The short chief had a bulldog face. He walked like a bulldog too, the heft of his chest lifted into the air, legs straight. When he arrived at the podium, he stood on the first step leading up to the Ferguson's front door. "We are doing all we can to find the Ferguson's boy. We ask every citizen–"

"Excuse me!"

The Chief of Police whuffed in surprise as an older woman marched forward, pushing through the edge of the crowd. There were several chuckles and laughs of shocked surprise at the woman's appearance. The beautiful print blouse, the giant, possibly-snakeskin purse, and the firefighter's pants and heavy boots. Cameras focused on her, every camera man's instincts screaming that *here* was a story.

"Pardon me, young man," the odd woman said, apparently not noting the white hair under the Chief's hat. "There's been a man in the park the last several weeks. I've only ever seen him in the shadow of the picnic shelter. He's nearly as tall as this here fella–" She looked a nearby rumple-suited man up and down. Nodding to confirm her own estimate, she added-while drawing one finger from her temple to her chin," And he has a scar on his face."

In the hotel room, the big man in the chair sat up straight. On the screen, the man in the rumpled brown suit was leaning down, speaking with Mrs. St. G. The man lifted his arm, as if inviting her to step away from the crowd.

"Mr. Ferguson!" a lady reporter called out from the crowd. "Did the mention of the scar mean something to you? You went quite pale."

Mr. Ferguson *was* quite pale. The smattering of freckles across his cheeks were a dark constellation. He attempted to pass off his reaction as, "the stress we are under." But none of the reporters missed the significant look he and his wife gave each other.

Another reporter held his phone in the air, screen toward the Fergusons. "Says here you have an older brother. Seamus. *He* has a scar on the side of his face. Why would your own brother kidnap your child?"

In the gloomy hotel room, the big man in the chair looked at the bound and hurting boy on the bed. For a moment, uncle and nephew looked into each other's eyes while the flickering blue light of the TV danced on the uncle's scarred face,

THEY HAD QUESTIONED HER FOR an hour.

"What was the man with the scar wearing?"

"What exactly was he doing in the park and in what locations had she noticed him?"

"Had he been smoking? Drinking coffee? Taking photographs? Reading?"

The short Chief of Police had joined the detective in the

rumpled brown suit who had called in Officers Greaves and Todd to recount the interview they had conducted with Mrs. St. G. Afterward, the detective had offered to drive her home, but she had seen the weariness and the focus in his eyes. He finally had a lead and he wanted to get on it. Firm fingers raked through messy brown hair with just a glint of copper in it. It was a touch too long, as if the detective had put off getting it cut one too many times. That hair fell over shockingly blue eyes that stood out all the more because of his bronze skin.

If he took better care of himself, well…. She had several grand and great grandnieces—and a nephew, come to think of it—that would appreciate the detective *and* demands of the detective's job. St. Georges understood atypical job descriptions.

His name was Knight—just Knight. When he gave her a card so she could call him with any details she might remember, the card had read, "Detective F. C. Knight." She wondered what the" F" and the "C" stood for. Her instincts were finely honed after a long life as a St. George and she fully expected to one day discover the names attached to those initials.

Those instincts were also loudly and firmly declaring that the man with the scar was playing some sort of game. A game he would want to control. So, Mrs. St. G went home.

She opened various and sundry cabinets, cupboards, and drawers, pulling items out as needed, packing her *...snakeskin? Alligator skin?* purse in preparation for a kidnapping.

SEAMUS FERGUSON STOOD WITHIN THE shadow of the hedges. His shoulders hunched like the shoulders of an angry vulture as he watched the house. Lights were on in some of the house's many windows, casting pools of warm light out onto the travesty of a lawn. Seamus hesitated to approach the house for fear he'd step in one of those odd holes.

The driveway was well-lit by tall, glass-enclosed lamps around which bronze dragons were wrapped. Odd decoration for a batty old biddy. The lamps lit the drive too well for an approach from that direction. It may have been possible to circle around through the park and approach the house from the rear, but he feared the back lawns were as filled with mounds of dirt and holes as were the front and side yards.

Why did the old bat do it? Dig the holes? Did she have an

archeologist complex? Did she really consider all those bits and pieces treasure to be hidden? That she was stark, raving crazy, he had no doubt. He had seen here in–

There she was now. Leaving her house. Locking the door. Placing the key in her extra-large, shiny green purse. Clomping down her front steps in those ridiculous boots. She moved spryly for a woman of her age, practically trotting down the long drive.

Seamus hunched his shoulders higher and held his breath as the old bat came along the sidewalk. Though the hedge separated them, he didn't want her to hear him. Not that she would. As usual, she kept up a continuous stream of muttered words, tsking and clicking her tongue.

"Sully, Sully. Where have you gone? Naughty boy, Mummy isn't happy about this. Where are you?"

Seamus's head swung slowly from right to left as she passed by. Dark eyes under thick brows seeking any movement though he couldn't see through the hedge. Then she passed beyond the end of the hedge.

Placing his feet carefully, he stalked along behind the old woman, remaining in the shadows of the trees.

AS MRS. ST. G TURNED FROM THE sidewalk and into the park, a car approached from the opposite direction, its headlights carving a bright curve in the gloomy evening as the vehicle took the turn in the road. The lights just missed her.

A few moments later, the car passed beneath the streetlight beside the park's entrance. It was a plain brown car so ordinary most people would not be able to say much about it. It was a car. It was brown. Had four doors.

If the driver had turned his head, he would have seen her. But he was focused on the road ahead and missed the sight of Mrs. St. G talking to the trees as she left the pool of lamplight and took the path toward the pond.

THE OLD BAT REMOVED A small flashlight out of her purse and shone the dull light around the twilight gloom. Peering at the bushes and the low hanging tree limbs. Seamus snorted quietly. The batteries in her light were so weak, if she shone it in his face, he wouldn't even blink.

She hadn't stopped talking to... who– or what– ever she was

talking to. Muttering on about "disappointing Mummy" and "no bisky-treats for you," while she trotted deeper into the dark shadows beneath the trees.

Clutching tightly to the burlap bag and roll of duct tape in his hand, the big man followed.

LIGHTS WERE ON IN SEVERAL rooms, but the room behind the front door was dark. Detective Knight pressed the doorbell a second time, *feeling* the beautiful song the bells rolled out.

No one answered.

He "bumped" the door… just to see if it would swing open of its own accord. He'd have no problems entering the house uninvited to check on its owner. She lived by herself, and the world was full of terrible things.

His eyes swept the tidy, if decoratively painted front porch before he jogged down the front steps. A walkway—flagstone with inset star blazes—led to the drive which went up past the house to a ramshackle two car garage deep enough to hold four. On the way, another walkway branched off, leading to the back porch.

As the detective headed toward the back door, he sensed... *something* from the garage behind him. A spot between his shoulder blades began to itch and his hand drifted of its own accord toward the sidearm concealed by his rumpled suit jacket.

He second guessed his reaction. He was tired. That's all it was. Exhaustion from running after dead-end leads. Seamus Ferguson was dead. Died in a car wreck ten years before. So, they were back to where they'd started.

He'd stopped by to see if Mrs. St. G could remember any-thing, anything at all that would give them a new lead.

The wood of the stairs creaked as he went up them. There was a rocker on the back porch. A white... hold up, that wasn't wood. He touched the edge of the chair back with his hand. Cold like metal. One more odd thing in a truly odd day. Who used metal rocking chairs? The entire time he had been interviewing Mrs. St. George, he'd tried to figure her out. She was odd and fierce and... well, some might say a bit batty. But she was just the type of older woman he'd love for an aunt.

It would be. They'd sit in the rockers. Lookout over the... lawn. Maybe he could help her level off some of the piles of dirt he saw in the warm glow of the house lights. He walked along the porch railing—it felt rough in spots—squinting his eyes to peer at the dirt heaps, trying to estimate how many there were. More than he could level in a day.

Afterward, she'd pour them tall glasses of lemonade. He wondered if she was the type of aunt who served cookies, too.

Thick, soft choco– He stopped mid-thought as he saw the freezer wrapped in huge chains. With a shot of cold through his gut, he came to terms with the fact that Mrs. St. George might be more than old, and fierce, and batty. She might just be criminally insane. That chest freezer was the perfect size to hide a young boy. And chain and padlock looked wickedly evil.

The detective ran off the porch toward his car. He should call this in. Get a warrant. Get backup. But if the boy was in the freezer... he could be out of time. Any delay could be deadly. Knight opened his trunk and flipped up the latch of the large toolbox where he expected to find his bolt cutters. They weren't there. Todd had borrowed them when they'd needed to rescue the horded Chihuahuas.

What to do?

He was reaching for his phone as he turned from the trunk of the car, picking up a flashlight as he did so. The garage.... It was another place one could hide a boy and it might just hold a pair of bolt cutters.

Ignoring the pricking feeling he felt along his skin, he jogged toward the ramshackle building. There was a side door and he––

What was that?

He stopped in his tracks and held his breath.

A faint scratching. The rattle of the garage door. As if something inside was trying to lift it up. Knight ran to the side door. A metal door. A cinderblock garage.

Whoever was inside bumped against the door. The unknown someone growled in a squeaky sort of way.

"Topher?" Knight shouted. "Stand back!" He inhaled, preparing to throw himself at the door.

TOPHER FERGUSON JERKED AWAKE AS something was dropped on the bed beside him. He'd been so deeply asleep that he'd failed to hear the door open at his uncle's return. His supposedly dead uncle.

He blinked as his uncle snapped on the crooked yellow-brown lamps above the bed.

That something—that someone—that had been dropped on

the bed was not much bigger than he. Her head was covered in a burlap bag, but the flowered blouse and the firefighter's pants were unmistakable.

Mrs. St. G's arms, big handbag stuck in the crook of one elbow, had been duct tape across her body, as if her abductor had dropped the bag over her head, stuck the end of the tape on one arm, and spun the petite, old woman around and around.

She smelled like lilac powder, charcoal, and chocolate chip cookies,

His uncle chewed out indecipherable words as he stomped around. He didn't pause as he pulled out his big knife from the duffel bag where he'd stashed it.

The boy clenched his jaw to keep from reacting. The spot where his finger was missing began to ache like the pounding of a drum. Mrs. St. G hadn't moved, and he was scared for her. Scared for himself.

He looked from the flash of light on the blade of the knife to the face of his uncle. Fear, dread, and betrayal churned in his stomach.

His uncle stretched out a large hand. Stretched it toward Mrs. St. G's head and Topher made a strangled noise of protest in the back of his throat. But Uncle Seamus ignored him and pulled the bag off the old woman's head.

She was staring at the knife-wielding man as if she had been able to see him through the burlap. Her eyes burned with a cold five. She didn't break her gaze as she asked, "Are you well, young Topher?"

Topher nodded.

Uncle Seamus lifted his blade. "Quiet you or it's– " He panto-mimed drawing the blade across his throat. "I'll do it." Somewhere outside, a car door slammed, catching his attention. He turned away, going over to peer through the blinds.

Topher looked up at Mrs. St. G who was watching him. To his surprise, she winked.

Inside his pocket, the sleeping dragon woke up.

DETECTIVE KNIGHT HAD JUST BRACED himself for the for-ward thrust and the impact against the door when the flashlight illuminated a key hanging on a small hook near the top of the doorframe. It fit the lock, and half a breath later, he was push-ing open the door. He hadn't gotten it more than a foot when it was ripped out of his hand as *something* shoved its way out of the garage.

The something—a seething, noisy, unidentifiable mass—separated into many somethings and the detective blinked hard, sweeping his flashlight back and forth, trying to make out what it was he was really seeing.

His light caught on and reflected off of scales—SCALES!

And wings.

Dragons!? It *couldn't* be. Just how sleep deprived was he?

But the growling, hissing, sparkling, scrabbling confusion of several dozen different dragon species was racing away from him. A few members of the little horde were flying.

Knight ran after the multicolored mass of mythical creatures. They were fast.

They were halfway down the drive by the time he'd gotten to his car. Wondering what he was doing, while at the same time *not thinking about it*, he folded himself into his car. The engine grumbled to life and he pushed the accelerator to the floor.

At the end of the drive, the confusion of small dragons made a hard left, some of their little legs slipping and sliding, or scratching the pavement as they dug claws in for purchase. Tires squealing, Knight followed.

DID HE TELL YOU WHY he's doing this?"

Topher Ferguson shook his head in response to Mrs. St. G's question. He wasn't sure why Uncle Seamus hadn't gagged her, but he was glad about that. He was both unspeakably terrified for her and deeply comforted that she was here.

He was further comforted by Sully.

The little dragon—about the size of Tohper's hand—had walked up Topher's leg and stomach, ruffling iridescent, periwinkle wings as he did so. His snout ended in a curved beak which matched the curve of his talons that had lightly poked through the boy's tee shirt.

As he crept closer to Mrs. St. G, Sully kept his eyes on Uncle Seamus. Large, ocean-blue orbs glittered with lighter blue flecks scattered among deep purple and forest green. There was a look in those big eyes—a look that said the pacing man should be thankful he, Lord Beryl Sultane Hanover Thwackston, aka Sully, was not full-sized,

The dragon crawled down between Topher and Mrs. St. G, close to her elbow crooked through the handbag's handles, and began trying to pry open the handbag. Topher assumed the little guy was trying to get at the charcoal biscuits Mr. St. G kept inside.

"He should know." Mrs. St. G stared at Uncle Seamus who didn't say anything despite his earlier knife waving.

The large man sat in the chair near the television. It creaked as he settled into it, propping on ankle on the other knee and picked at fingernail with the point of his knife.

Mrs. St. G looked down at Topher. He could see his own, faint reflection in her spectacles that had surprisingly remained on her nose during her kidnapping. His hair was as thick as his mothers, curls not as tight. They were looser. Wilder. Red, like his father's. His dusty brown skin came from his beautiful and smart mother.

"He's using you." Mrs. St. G softened the words with an apologetic smile, but she didn't believe in sugar coating things. Topher liked that about her.

He tried to ask how his uncle was using him, the sock muffled the words.

"I imagine it's something to do with your father. That is, unfortunately, how these things go."

Uncle Seamus snorted and lowered his knife. Topher shuddered as it arced down through the air. "What would you know about 'these things,' old woman?"

"My name is Mrs. St. George, and I know 'bout families and history. The dragons that haunt us."

Uncle Seamus didn't say anything.

Mrs. St. G shifted on the bed, flexing her arms. Topher understood. He was tired of laying here, too. His uncle had given him two bathroom breaks, but always rebound him and tossed him on the bed.

"What haunts you Seamus Ferguson?"

Uncle Seamus stood up, tossing the knife into the duffle and digging out a silver flask. After unscrewing the cap, he lifted it to his lips and took a long drink. "Nothin'." He spat the word out as he lowered the flask. "Nothin' haunts me, lady."

He spun on his heel, the lamplight falling on his scar. It stood out angry and yellow on his face as he stared down Mrs. St. G. "*I* do the haunting."

"Your brother give you that scar?" she asked conversationally.

"Stop asking questions." Uncle Seamus returned the flask to the duffel, exchanging it for a thick mobile phone with a stubby antenna as big as Topher's finger.

"Hmmph." Mrs. St. G wiggled her arms again. "The words are damming up behind your lips. Wanting to spill out. To tell the boy why he brought this upon himself."

"He didn't bring this on himself. His mother did—" Uncle Seamus cut off his words, shaking a large finger. "Clever, aren't you?"

"Cleverer than you. They'll catch you, you know?"

Sully squirmed around, his wings poking Topher who bit the sock in order to keep from wincing in surprise.

"Nope, lady, they won't. I've got a plan."

Mrs. St. G flexed her arms again, pushing gently at the duct tape binding her. "What are you going to do with us?"

Uncle Seamus didn't respond. He glanced down at the phone, brushing his thumb across the on switch but not pushing it.

"I'm sorry, young Topher. Your uncle plans on killing us."

"No." Uncle Seamus lifted his head. "At least not the boy."

"Why?" Topher asked. The sock muffled the word. He was asking why Mrs. St. G and not him, but his uncle understood the distorted word, not his meaning.

"I want your mother, your father, to remember. Every time they see your hand, I want them to remember."

Topher felt his eyes watering again. He didn't understand what Uncle Seamus meant, but his words made Topher cry. He sniffed as some of the tears trickled down into his nose.

"Dry it up, kid. You'll survive. Have a story to tell. At least it wasn't your own father who gave you your scars." Uncle Seamus trailed a finger down his cheek, along the bumps and puckered skin there. "Now...."

Uncle Seamus reached over and withdrew a slip of paper from his duffel. The paper was folded in half. He flipped it open and laid it on the table, then pressed the on button for the phone. It was while he was focused on punching in the number that Mrs. St. G took a deep breath and flexed her arms again, pushing them out to the side as hard as she could.

Her left arm broke free.

Uncle Seamus turned at the sound caused by duct tape coming away from her skin. With a snarl, he leaped for the bed but... something attacked his face just as something else—something strange and weird that hissed and honked and growled—thudded against the door.

Topher, eyes wide, tried to watch both his uncle and Mrs. St. G.

As Uncle Seamus had come toward the bed, Sully had jumped, latching onto his face. Uncle Seamus shouted, stumbling back. He slapped at his face in a wild manner but gave no indication he could see what was currently biting his ear.

Mrs. St. G struggled with the duct tape that had teeny, tiny punctures in it. Did Sully chew it? As something hit the door a second time while making a terrible racket, she managed to disentangle her arm. She fumbled the clasp to her purse.

"What are you doing to me?" Uncle Seamus shook his head, trying to shake off the little dragon that was run around and round his skull, staying just out of reach. Scratch marks from Sully's talons bled thin lines. "I'll kill you! I'll—"

Uncle Seamus reached behind himself. Dug in the duffle. Came up with a knife.

Mrs. St. G reached into her handbag. Withdrew a crossbow. And shot Uncle Seamus in the leg.

The door burst open and the man in the rumpled brown suit came in, gun in hand, falling against the wall as the hissing, growling horde got underfoot. Sully roar—a small roar from a small dragon—but the horde responded, throwing themselves at the howling man who was hopping around on one leg, clutching at the crossbow bolt with one hand while trying to catch Sully with the other.

Anxious Frank honked a growl as he ran circles around Seamus's hopping leg. Then he farted. The room filled up with a hideous, burning stench.

Just as she got near Seamus' face, Flit sneezed a loogy of fire fluid, hiccupping almost simultaneously. And the loogy exploded in a miniature cloud of fire.

THE LEMONADE WAS NOT TOO sweet. Not too sour. Cold and freshly made. The detective had not had to shovel piles of dirt to earn a glass. And, there were cookies. Soft with plenty of chocolate chips and the light taste of cinnamon.

"Topher recovering well?" Mrs. St. G asked.

They were sitting at a little metal table on two metal chairs on her back porch. She had fed the horde little charcoal biscuit treats and then tossed a handful of Christmas tinsel into the back yard. The members of the horde were dashing around trying to secure strands of tinsel for themselves while stealing more from others. Surprisingly, there were no nasty, low down, dirty fights between the dragons.

Dragons! He still couldn't believe it. Couldn't believe he had followed a horde of house pet-sized mythical reptiles to a crime scene.

The official story they had told was that after Mrs. St. G shot Seamus Ferguson with her crossbow—which had been confiscated—she had called him.

"He'll be fine." Knight took another bite of cookie.

"His mother choose his father over Seamus?" Mrs. St. G touched Sully's tail. The dragon was curled up on her shoulder, snoring softly.

He swallowed the cookie down with lemonade before answering. "Something like that. Seems the brothers were always competing with each other. A car accident allowed Seamus to start a new life. Such as it was. He just couldn't let go." They were quiet for a moment, staring at the sneaky little dragons playing take away from each other.

"That conflict started before them. Their father. Probably their father's father and on back. The things we leave behind, the inheritances... they are more than the treasures on our shelves and the money in our vaults. Speaking of things we leave behind." She tilted her head and lifted an eyebrow. "That young Topher will make an excellent St. George when he is grown. But I need someone to fill in until then."

"He's a Ferguson, Mrs. St. G. And, no offense, but you can't adopt him."

She waved a veined hand in dismissal. "We all come to the name of St. George with other names. Other lives, first. But we all have the Sight. *You* have the Sight."

"What's your point?" Knight leaned back in his chair.

"There are dragons in the world. And, yes, the St. Georges are known for slaying them. But they only slew the ones who deserved it—the ones who preyed on the weak and vulnerable. Those who have borne the name of St. George have spent their lives protecting the innocent and speaking up for those who could not speak for themselves. I believe, detective, that you might have some experience doing the same."

"What exactly are you asking me to do?"

"Learn how to be St. George. And then pass the knowledge along to the boy when he's grown up, should I not live that long."

Flit landed on the table and leaned toward his plate. She'd wrapped a piece of tinsel around one of her little horns and now seemed focused on his cookie. He carefully held the uneaten piece to her. Delicately, she sunk buried her tiny teeth into the edge and ripped a chunk off.

"I'm not saying yes, but if I did, what would I need to do?"

Mrs. St. G stood up without disturbing Sully. "Well, Detective F.C. Knight.... To begin with, allow me to introduce you to my house. Oh, and you might want to buy a pair of fire fighter's pants at your earliest convenience."

ABOUT THE AUTHORS

Tracy Eire has been a professional writer for almost a decade writing to a variety of needs, from the magazine Beautiful Bizarre, to collaborations with artists like Jenny Boot. In the mid-2000s, she started her art career and fiction publications. An oil painter with interest in watercolour painting, she was creatively influenced by her childhood home of Newfoundland. The wildness, mysticism, and kindness of this Northern island home just a step out of time, translated into optimism and depictions of light in art. The stamp of those wild climes and pagan survivals became strong impulses in her writing. They can be seen from her rich cast of mystical characters, to the haunting moments we all experience to one side of the flow of normal life, captured in her books. A seasoned writer, she's neurodiverse. Overcoming her disabilities with grit and flexibility creates a highly individual point of view in her work.

Please visit her at <u>tracyeire.site</u>

N.D. GRAY once dreamed of being an astronaut. Now, she writes about characters who reach for the stars. She also writes for children under the name Naomi Glasarth.

When she's not writing, she works full time as a caregiver specializing in adults with I/DD, hangs out with the pup pack, and enjoys several creative pursuits, including acrylic painting.

Please visit her at ndgray.com

ELIZABETH KNOLLSTON has always been an avid reader of science fiction and fantasy. Now she works on turning her vivid imagination of alien worlds, long lost secrets of the universe, mystical realms and the obligatory dragon into stories of her own. Often blending religious questions and an abiding love for archeology into the driving forces behind her worlds. When not daydreaming about why the local pet store doesn't carry baby dragons, or being a part of a manned mission to Mars, Elizabeth teaches therapeutic riding, spends time with her dog, works in the garden, and loves giving back to the community.

Heidi Moone writes things. She says, "I've started to publish some of these things to share them with others. I like writing stories about fantastic places and the magic in the everyday world. I've been reading, and writing, from an early age, and I come from a tradition of oral storytellers, in rural Newfoundland. I love the written word, and it's my favorite medium to communicate my ideas to anyone looking for a new world to explore, and new people to meet along the way."

Please visit her at **heidimoone.com**

Karli Stites is a tech nerd by day (and also by night), so she did the only thing she could when faced with an overload of creativity that had nowhere to go: she started writing sci-fi and fantasy novels. Karli published the first book in her debut series, Edge of Destruction, in 2019 and the space opera trilogy will be completed in 2021. A lover of all things fantasy and mythological, Karli was excited to dive into the world of dragons and intends to expand her dragonverse further in the future.

Check out her website at karlistitesauthor.com to join her newsletter and keep an eye on upcoming releases!

FOR MORE INFORMATION
PLEASE VISIT US AT
NDGRAY.COM/MINITHOLOGY

www.ingramcontent.com/pod-product-compliance
Lightning Source LLC
Chambersburg PA
CBHW070939190726
48292CB00004B/1244